CHAMELEON PLANET

A posthumous collaboration between John Russell Fearn and his biographer Philip Harbottle, and based on Fearn's last written notes, *Chameleon Planet* picks up the saga directly following the ending of Fearn's *Earth Divided* (Golden Amazon saga # 20) when the Cosmic Crusaders prepare to pursue their enemy Karg into space, in a desperate race to recover the Amazon's spaceship, the *Ultra*!

After almost plunging into the sun, the Amazon and Abna are flung countless light years to a truly fantastic solar system, where a planet orbits a black hole—with devastating effects on the planet's life and Time itself! Meanwhile, the remaining Crusaders, Viona, Mexone and Thania, explore a different planetary system—and find themselves threatened by an ancient alien vampire!

THE GOLDEN AMAZON SAGA

CHAMELEON PLANET

THE GOLDEN AMAZON SAGA, BOOK 21

JOHN RUSSELL FEARN
and PHILIP HARBOTTLE

WILDSIDE PRESS

CHAMELEON PLANET

CONTENTS

THE GOLDEN AMAZON SERIES

by Philip Harbottle

Followers of John Russell Fearn's "Golden Amazon" series may be surprised to discover that they have yet another Amazon novel to enjoy—CHAMELEON PLANET, book #21 in this present series Yet in my preface to the previous volume, EARTH DIVIDED, I informed readers that the novel was Fearn's last—and not only his last "Amazon" novel, but quite literally, the last thing he ever wrote before his sudden and unexpected death from a heart attack, aged only 52.

So where has *Chameleon Planet* come from, and why does it bear Fearn's name as well as my own? For the answers, read on!

My life-long interest and study of Fearn's work has particularly intensified in recent years when, as his literary executor, I decided to retype into my computer scores of his novels and stories to take advantage of the internet as a medium for offering them to publishers, especially in the U.S.A, and to Gary Lovisi's Small Press, Gryphon Books in particular. This created new opportunities for their reprinting, or, as in the case of his later Golden Amazon novels, first book publication. And as I retyped and edited his stories, it gave me a detailed insight into Fearn's style and methods of story construction.

In 2000, in my capacity as a literary agent, I succeeded in reselling reprint rights to London publishers Robert Hale for every one of Fearn's many paperback westerns. Hale subsequently issued the first-ever hardcover editions of these westerns, and also first-published a couple of hitherto unpublished western novels, which I had revised and edited from Fearn's original mss.

But when, after some two-dozen titles, the supply of Fearn western novels to reprint ran out, I hit on the idea of trying to write my own western novels, based upon a number of Fearn's western *short stories*. In this I was essentially emulating Fearn's own technique, which he had employed with some of his early science fiction pulp magazine short stories, when he later turned them into paperback novels.

As copyright holder—by virtue of Mrs. Fearn's Will— I was entitled to do this. So, by taking a couple of disparate western short stories, and then revising them to incorporate the same characters, and expanding them to novel length, I found I could produce a pretty good pastiche—certainly good enough for Hale to publish. And since these collaborative novels were later reprinted in paperback by yet another publisher, F.A. Thorpe, they must have had something going for them…

So, once the supply of original Fearn Golden Amazon stories had finally ran out, I decided to see if I could reprise my western technique to create a new Golden Amazon science fiction novella in the same way! After studying many of his stories, I finally selected two totally unconnected Fearn short SF stories, "Chameleon Planet" (1940) and "Destroyer from the Past"(1942)—neither of them an

Amazon story—and then revised and expanded them with new material of my own to novella length, replacing their original characters with the Cosmic Crusaders. The result is the book you are now reading! (Some readers might be interested to seek out the *original* version of "Chameleon Planet", which can be found in the recent Borgo new Fearn sf collection, *World Without Chance*.)

In writing this story, I followed the pattern of the final phase of the Amazon, and wrote the story to novella length.

Chameleon Planet is thus a genuine posthumous collaboration between Fearn and myself. Its opening scene is, in fact, based on a very short note Fearn made at the end of the original mss of his last Amazon novel, *Earth Divided*. His notation referred to the beginning of the next story he had hoped to write.

At the conclusion of *Earth Divided*, Karg, the Crusaders' sworn enemy had escaped from Earth in a spaceship, and was heading for the Ultra, the Crusaders' mighty space machine—which they had been tricked into abandoning in deep space. Fearn's novel ended with the Amazon exclaiming: "We've got to stop him!"

For more than 40 years, fans of the Amazon—myself amongst them—had been wondering 'what happened next?' With *Chameleon Planet* I have given my version of events, as I adjudged Fearn might have written them had he not been cruelly struck down with a heart attack.

Chameleon Planet, when it appeared from Gryphon Books in 2005, was therefore the first new Golden Amazon story to appear since 1961 (excluding, of course, Fearn's own two previously unpublished Amazon stories *Lords of Creation* and *Duel With Colossus*), both now currently available in this new Borgo Books series. But things might well have been entirely different!

Something that was not widely known is that *Star Weekly* editor Gwen Cowley instigated a serious attempt to find another writer to continue the series, after Fearn's death. She wrote to Mrs. Fearn on May 30, 1963:

"Dear Mrs. Fearn:

I was in New York recently and called on the Scott Meredith Literary Agency who asked if I would write to you inquiring if you would be interested in making a little extra money by selling the rights to use the character "The Golden Amazon" in some stories that they may be bringing out along science-fiction lines. They felt this was too good a character to let die. You might like to write directly to them and if so I would suggest that you address your letter to Mr. Henry Morrison, Scott Meredith Literary Agency, 580 Fifth Avenue, New York 36, NY. I am sending them a copy of this letter so that they will know I have written you.

You will want to follow through, I imagine, one way or the other.

With very best wishes, I am,

Yours sincerely,

Gwen Cowley,
Fiction Editor.

Mrs. Fearn wrote positively to Scott Meredith on June 4th, 1963, but her letter crossed in the post with one sent direct to her by Henry Morrison, the agency's Vice-President, and dated the same day:

Dear Mrs. Fearn,

I've just received a copy of Gwen Cowley's letter to you dated of May 30th, and I wanted to write to you immediately to clarify one point.

We're not suggesting that you sell the rights to THE

GOLDEN AMAZON. Miss Cowley told me that they still receive a good many letters asking about THE GOLDEN AMAZON, and it struck me as a good idea for us to suggest that we have one of our clients take over your character and write further novels about her—and split the monies between you and our author. We've done this in several other instances where the original author has passed away, and the normal split is 25% to the owner of the rights (in this case yourself) and 75% to the writer (who of course has to do all the work). This has been rather profitable in the past, and I think it would be true of the present situation.

 I hope that you'll give this suggestion serious consideration, and we'll look forward to word from you.

 Sincerely,

Henry Morrison.

Mrs. Fearn readily agreed to this proposal, and so through the Scott Meredith Literary Agency in America, some of their leading client—including in particular A. Bertram Chandler and Robert Silverberg—were tried out to continue the Amazon series. Unfortunately, it would appear that none of these writers were adequately made aware of what had gone before, and of the true nature and history of the Amazon. Their attempts to write new Amazon novels were therefore all rejected. Chandler's, in particular, whilst excellent in themselves, were hopelessly flawed because his friend Donald H. Tuck had sent him copies of the original "prototype" Golden Amazon stories that had been published in *Fantastic Adventures*, for his guidance. Tuck had only been intending to help, but his intervention proved to be disastrous. The *Fantastic Adventures* Amazon and the *Star Weekly* Amazon were *completely different characters*! Although Tuck had been in correspondence with me for some time regarding Fearn's data for the reference book he was compiling, *The Handbook of Science Fiction*, (on which I was also helping him generally) he had not thought to consult me first. I regret to say that I was unable to forgive him for this, and after I had written somewhat intemperately to express my dismay—rather unfairly claiming he had unwittingly deprived Mrs. Fearn of possible royalties she sorely needed—we never corresponded again. I regret that very much.

However, both Chandler and Silverberg were invited to convert their attempts into "straight" non-Amazon SF novels, which the *Star Weekly* later published. These novels were subsequently reprinted by Ace Books in 1964, as *The Coils of Time* and *One of our Asteroids is Missing*—naturally, without any attribution to the Golden Amazon, or payment to Mrs. Fearn.

Had they succeeded with their first efforts, I am quite sure that with the Amazon remaining visible and in print in the *Star Weekly*, then Fearn's own later Amazon novels would have been reprinted in book form much earlier (quite possibly by Ace, who were regularly featuring both Chandler and Silverberg at this time), and certainly in the lifetime of Fearn's widow.

Carrie Fearn was to live until 1982, 22 years after her late husband, and it is a tragedy that she did not benefit from Fearn's best literary creation. Under the agreement with the *Star Weekly*, and Henry Morrison of the Scott Meredith agency, Mrs. Fearn would have received 25% of the proceeds of any new novel. It was money she sorely needed: as a freelance writer, Fearn had died without a personal pension.

It was therefore of considerable satisfaction to me that

(after she appointed me her agent) that I was able to supplement Mrs. Fearn's meagre state pension in having many of his 'Vargo Statten' SF novels translated and reprinted in Italy during the 1970s. Their surprising success eventually led to the reprinting throughout the following decade of a number of his western and detective novels in Italy also—too late, alas, for Mrs. Fearn to benefit.

But at least the proceeds of these later sales were able to benefit my daughter Claire, eventually helping to finance her through University—which was entirely in accordance with Mrs. Fearn's wishes. On learning of Claire's birth in 1972, she had added a special codicil to her Will bequeathing all Fearn's copyrights to me. Childless herself, she became very fond of my daughter, who came to know her as "Auntie" Carrie.

And now events have moved full circle—with a vengeance! Today, more and more of Fearn's wonderful science fiction, western and detective stories are being returned to print, nicely in time to benefit my own grandchildren, Eleanor Rose King and her younger brother, Arthur Philip King. I suspect that Mrs. Fearn would have liked that, as perhaps would have Fearn himself (his own mother was also called Rose).

Fearn died childless, but the daughter of his imagination, Violet Ray Brant—the Golden Amazon—lives on. With *Chameleon Planet* I hope I have managed to capture and retain something of the essence of the Golden Amazon, and how well I have succeeded—or failed—is up to you, the reader, to judge. At the very least, I was able to untangle the untidy loose ends Fearn left dangling, and so made it possible at last for further new exploits of the Amazon and her fellow Cosmic Crusaders to be written.

This time, however, that task fell to my own Cosmos Literary Agency, so I was able to provide my clients with full details of the real Amazon and sample novels. These details were sent to Brian Ball, John Glasby and E.C. 'Ted' Tubb, all of whom had expressed interest. Unfortunately both Brian and Ted fell victims to ill-health and were unable to submit their versions of the Amazon—but John Glasby came through brilliantly, and he was able to write further new adventures of the Cosmic Crusaders for Gryphon Books. It is hoped that these further adventures may be appearing from Wildside Press at some future date.

Watch for further announcements!

CHAPTER ONE

Pursuit through space

Beyond the Earth three spaceships were speeding through the void, all of them following the same course.

In the leading ship, which was far outstripping the other two, were three of the famed Cosmic Crusaders, the superhuman band of space rovers whose intervention on their return from interstellar space had recently freed the Earth from tyranny. Viona, daughter of the Golden Amazon, Viona's husband Mexone, and the orphaned Thania, the latest recruit and youngest member of the team. Both Mexone and Thania had once been inhabitants of other worlds visited by the original trio of Crusaders.

In the second vessel was Karg, former leader of the Pagans on Earth, and now a fugitive from vengeful justice. The third ship, now rapidly gaining on Karg, held Violet Ray Brant, more generally known as the Golden Amazon, together with her husband Abna, a seven foot blond giant. A descendant of Atlantis, he was joint leader of the Crusaders, together with his fabulous wife.

The Amazon was at the space radio as Abna piloted the third vessel. "Amazon calling Viona. Are you aligned to your target star yet?"

"Yes, Mother. Mexone's just downloading the co-ordinates into our central computer now. And Thania has set the automatic pilot for our jump to hyperspace when we reach a speed approaching that of light. Once we reach that target star, we'll be close to where we left the Ultra. Another short hop after that, and we'll reach it."

"What about Karg's ship?" the Amazon questioned. "Have you overtaken him yet?"

"Yes, we've already passed him: he was traveling on the same trajectory as us, heading out of the solar system. I don't mind admitting I was tempted to slow down and blast him with what armaments our ship has!"

"No, that's our job, Viona—and our ship is equipped for the job. Your father and I will deal with him. Your task is to accelerate at the fastest possible speed, and get to the Ultra before Karg, or anyone else for that matter. That's why I sent you on ahead."

"Yes, we're beginning to feel the strain of our constant acceleration. We'll have to sign off soon now, and retire to the acceleration couches. The automatics will take over from there and accelerate us to light speed…"

"Which won't be long now, judging by the speed you're already making," Abna remarked, glancing at the instruments panel.

Within her own leading vessel, Viona sent her final message. "Viona signing off. Goodbye Mother—Father. Good luck in dealing with Karg. We'll be back for you in the Ultra as quickly as we can. But the Ultra's so far away it may take a couple of months."

The Amazon's brief reply came through after a short delay, testimony of the increasing distance between their two ships.

"Goodbye."

Viona switched off the space radio, and turned to her fellow Crusaders. "We're approaching our optimum speed. Time to prepare ourselves for the journey through hyperspace. Everything set, Mexone?"

"Everything," her husband assented. "The pre-set controls will divert our ship into hyperspace. We'd best relax in deep sleep since there's nothing to see in that limbo. When we've reached our target star we'll drop out into normal space, and instruments will awaken us."

Without any flicker of emotion Viona and Mexone moved to one side of the control room, where they settled themselves down on powerfully sprung beds, affixing themselves by instrument-studded straps at the sides, which they clicked into place. To them the tremendous journey ahead of them was purely a matter of routine, something they had done many times before. The teenage Thania, however, exhibited a definite tense excitement. Whilst in her short career as a Crusader, she had already traveled through hyperspace on several occasions, the situation still held elements of novelty.

Within seconds of their having settled themselves, the automatic controls gave the vessel a further mighty surge of acceleration. The trio lay motionless, even their superhuman bodies now beginning to feel the terrible dragging weight of constant acceleration upon them. Breathing became a Herculean effort...their surroundings seemed to swim and gyrate, becoming suffused with spinning lights that gradually faded into total blackness as the Crusaders deliberately let themselves slip into unconsciousness. Tiny hypodermic needles projected from the couch straps, injecting the Crusaders with a carefully calculated amount of a powerful narcotic. It would cause a state of suspended animation for the predetermined duration of their long flight through hyperspace.

"Goodbye." The Golden Amazon switched off the space radio, and relaxed back into the sprung seat at the spaceship's controls. She shot a sideways glance at her husband.

Abna smiled faintly. "Shouldn't that have been 'Au revoir', Vi?"

"That goes without saying!" the Amazon snapped, then she compressed her lips, annoyed with herself. It was not often—if at all—that the Golden Amazon revealed any emotions. And then it was only in an unusually dangerous situation that involved her daughter or husband, and to a slightly lesser extent her son in law Mexone, and the teenage girl Thania.

The present situation held danger in plenty. The Amazon and Abna, in their own second ship in pursuit of Karg's vessel, were involved in a duel that would end in death for one of them. There was also possible danger facing the other three Crusaders in their spaceship now speeding out of the solar system. Even when Viona's ship completed the long jump through hyperspace and reached their mighty space machine the Ultra, there was no guarantee that the vessel would still be space-worthy.

Many months had passed since they had been tricked into abandoning it in space, and been snatched across thousands of light years to their home planet, Earth. There, they had waged a fantastic battle to defeat Karg, the leader of the Pagans, so-called, who had held sway in one hemisphere of an Earth divided into two civilizations, the Normals and the Pagans.

Now the Pagans had been utterly defeated by the Cosmic Crusaders, and the Earth reunited. But Karg had managed to escape in a spaceship, armed with the co-ordinates in space where drifted the abandoned Ultra. He knew it to be stocked with all manner of deadly weapons, including the ultimate weapon—the Zero-Thought Amplifier.

If Karg succeeded in reaching the Ultra first, then he could return and lay waste to the Earth. Or could he? In the interval of time, the Ultra could easily have been damaged by some cosmic accident, or even seized by space marauders. As the Crusaders well knew from their voyages of exploration in the interstellar deeps, the vast Milky Way held many inhabited planets and space-faring civilizations.

"It's certainly fortunate that Earth scientists never managed to improve on our original Ultra's hyper-drive engines for their own spaceships," Abna remarked, turning from the screen where Karg's fleeing vessel showed as a tiny dot of light.

"Fortunate?" The Amazon was puzzled.

"If you recall, Vi, when we were snatched back to Earth in the duplicate Ultra, there was a long period of steady acceleration up to the speed of light before the hyper-drive cut in, and plunged us into hyperspace? You know why, of course?"

"Naturally I do," the Amazon said impatiently. "Once in hyperspace, the normal laws of space and motion do not apply. Any object, such as a spaceship, when entering hyperspace travels thousands of times faster than at the point of entry. So the faster a ship travels *before* it enters hyperspace, the greater the speed whilst *in* hyperspace. Unfortunately, whilst in hyperspace no further acceleration is possible, because normal laws don't apply. But if the speed at the time of entry is great enough, many light years can be travelled in a relatively short time. Journeys that would take years in normal space, where light speed is the limiting factor."

"Exactly," Abna said deliberately. "Which is why Viona and the others are able to beat Karg to the Ultra. Being superhuman, they can stand a greater degree of accelerative strain and reach a speed near to the speed of light long before he does… Ah!" Abna broke off, and gave a sigh of satisfaction. Whilst talking, he had been watching the instruments carefully.

"The contact signal with Viona's ship has been broken," he announced. "That means she has made the jump to hyperspace, and we've lost contact with her."

"Of which fact Karg will also be well aware," the Amazon said. "He has the same instruments aboard his vessel as we have." She looked at Abna, her eyes gleaming with satisfaction. "He must know now that he's beaten! If he were to go into hyperspace now, at his present sub-light speed, it would take him about a year to reach the Ultra."

"That's the point I was making, Vi. Karg *can't* escape into hyperspace now, in order to throw off our pursuit of him, even if he wanted to! The hyper drive, as we originally invented it for the first Ultra, was entirely automatic in its operation. It could only be activated when the ship approached to within a fraction of the speed of light, the fastest possible speed in the normal universe. Since then we've added refinements to our current Ultra to enable us to divert into hyperspace whenever we want, no matter what our speed is. That doesn't signify here," Abna finished, smiling broadly, "because these Earth spaceships have no such refinement."

"Which means we've got him!" the Amazon said triumphantly. "We're gaining on him steadily now because both of us can stand this present constant acceleration, and he can't—"

"Unless," Abna cut in, "he was to retire to his acceleration bunk and set the automatic controls for constant acceleration." He smiled grimly. "But that wouldn't do him any good, because he'd quickly become unconscious, and couldn't carry out any evasive maneuvers when we close in on him! Altogether, he's between the devil and the deep blue sea!"

"You take over here, Abna," the Amazon said, rising to her feet. "Keep accelerating until you've brought us within range of Karg's ship. I'll be on the protonic cannon—I want to be the one to personally blast Karg to atoms! He is unfit to live. I should have killed him back on Earth when he was my captive."

Abna said nothing, frowning slightly as he slid into the Amazon's vacated control chair. He did not share the Amazon's utterly ruthless disregard for human life. But he knew that, in this instance at least, that she was exactly right.

"Make sure you don't miss, Vi," he warned. "You've only one split-second shot as we come in behind him. He can't fire at us from behind of course, but the moment we flash ahead of him he can—and will—open fire on us, when our attacking positions will be reversed."

"I won't miss. Rely on it." The Amazon, now settled in the seat before the mighty protonic cannon, was already centering Karg's spaceship in the cross-hairs of her weapon. Then she gave a frown.

"Abna! What the devil are you playing at?" she cried sharply. "Karg's getting away! He's veered off course and is now traveling faster than us!"

CHAPTER TWO

Into the sun

"Only one answer, Vi." Abna gave a sideways glance at the Amazon as she came back across the control room and slid into the chair beside him. "He's set a new course, put in the automatic pilot, and retired to his acceleration couch. Now he's piling on as much acceleration as he can stand.

"It won't do him any good, though," Abna continued. "He's still way below light speed, and we can still follow him once we've worked out his new course—" Abna fell silent, giving his entire concentration to the instruments, and feeding the information constantly to the ship's computer.

Both he and the Amazon winced slightly with the strain of deceleration as the front reactors and side rockets blasted, slewing their machine round in a gradual arc to follow the new course Karg had taken.

"Well?" the Amazon demanded at length, her voice impatient. "Where's he headed? And more particularly, are we locked on to him and following his course?"

"Yes, we're locked on to him again—and gaining," Abna answered. "Though he now has quite a start on us, after that surprise move."

"But where's he headed? Surely he knows there's nowhere he can run to? We can catch up to him long before he reaches any of the nearest planets. They're scores of millions of miles away from this region of space."

"Believe it or not, Vi, he isn't headed for any of the planets," Abna answered slowly, studying his instruments intently. "If he stays on his present trajectory—and whilst he's still accelerating he can't do anything else—he's on an apparent collision course with the sun!"

"What!" the Amazon's voice was incredulous. "That doesn't make sense! Let me check your figures—"

Abna was thoughtful as the Amazon did so. "Perhaps it does make sense," he said slowly. "Realizing that he's beaten, maybe he's intending to commit an elaborate form of suicide by plunging into the sun?"

The Amazon glanced up, an odd gleam in her eyes. "You're right about his course, Abna, but wrong about his motive. And," she finished, smiling grimly, "he's just made the biggest mistake of his life!"

"Mistake?"

"Karg thinks he can trick us into following him. He expects us to accelerate to overtake him, and he's hoping that in doing so we'll be caught by the sun's gravity and utterly consumed in its outer atmosphere!"

"But surely he's running the same risk himself?"

"I don't believe so. What he has done—or rather his ship's computer has—is to calculate a course that will take him to the very demarcation line. By aiming to one side of the sun—going as near to it as he dares—and constantly accelerating, the result will be that he will swing around the sun in a vast arc, like a slingshot! The sun's own gravity will increase his speed considerably, and—judged correctly—it will be sufficient to fling him clear of the sun's gravity field before he burns up."

"I see. Yes, you're right, Vi," Abna breathed. "But *too much* speed approaching so near the sun, would mean that a following ship would be unable to pull clear in time! The devil! He's gambling on us following him at an even greater speed than his own—and being destroyed in the process! Well, that won't happen now that we're aware of it." Abna smiled and made to reach for the controls.

"All we need to do is to change course, accelerate, and go safely around the sun to its other side, and wait for Karg emerging in his slingshot orbit. Then blast him—"

"No!" The Amazon clamped a yellow hand on Abna's wrist in a vice-like grip, preventing him from resetting their course. "We can't do that! We've got to follow him!"

"Are you crazy, Vi?" Abna demanded. "We've just established that we'd be committing suicide that way!"

"You're not *thinking*, Abna!" the Amazon snapped, slowly releasing her iron grip on Abna's wrist. Had Abna been a normal man, his wrist would have been broken. He rubbed it absently, staring at her blankly.

"Don't you see?" the Amazon continued. "With the sun's gravity to help him, Karg is now building up his speed to very nearly that of the speed of light! As his ship swings around the sun, the moment it's aligned once more with the target star in the region of space where the Ultra is presently drifting, his automatic pilot will make the jump to hyperspace! He'll vanish from our space before we can get a shot at him!"

"By heaven, you're right, Vi!" Abna beat his great fist in frustration on the edge of the control panel. "That means he's outsmarted us! And," he finished bitterly, "at his eventual speed, he might even just beat Viona to the Ultra! Once aboard it, he can lie in wait and blast her ship to atoms. She'll not be expecting him to be there! We've no way of warning her, unless we travel there ourselves. But by the time we'd get there, it'll be too late!" He gave the Amazon a despairing look.

"Out of that control seat, Abna," the Amazon snapped. "I'm taking over. Don't you ever listen to me? I told you that Karg had made the greatest mistake of his life, didn't I? We're going to accelerate and follow him in to the sun, catch him up and blast him to atoms as we intended, and then—"

"I get it now!" Abna said, understanding and admiration for the Amazon's reasoning coming into his eyes. "You're intending to make a random jump to hyperspace yourself before we are consumed in the sun! Once in hyperspace we'll be safe from the sun. Then we can drop back into our own space before we've traveled too far, and head back to the solar system, to await Viona's return. A brilliant idea, Vi—but a mighty dangerous one! If we make the slightest miscalculation we've had it!"

"Then make sure that we don't!" the Amazon snapped. "Get busy on the computer and work out the details. Whilst you're doing that, I'll fix it for us to automatically enter hyperspace when we hit light speed just before we enter the sun's atmosphere. Just pray that it won't be too late!" The Amazon fell silent, struck by a sudden memory from the distant past.

Once before she had played tag with the sun's gravity—and won. On that occasion, she had been operating on her own, before she had met Abna. She had tricked an alien invasion armada into following her Ultra towards the sun.

Unable to pull free of the sun's gravity in time, the entire armada had been utterly consumed.

Her brilliant stratagem had saved the Earth from invasion, yes—but only to plunge it into an even greater danger. The sun itself had been thrown into a tremendous upheaval, and had begun a gradual collapse into a white dwarf. But then she had met Abna, and together they had performed a scientific miracle and succeeded in rekindling the sun… She gave a slight start, snapping out of her reverie as she felt Abna's arm slip around her shoulders.

As she glanced up he gave her a quick kiss.

"I know what you're thinking about, Vi," he said softly. "I'm remembering, too. It was the sun that first brought us together, wasn't it? But there's no way it's now going to burn us apart! We're going to win through again!"

* * * *

The sun.

A vast, seething sea of incandescent gas, a mighty globe of atomic fury. A gigantic boiling ocean of shimmering flame, of twisting and writhing energies. Here and there gaped the strange darker masses of eye-like sunspots, their edges shining brightly where the flocculi fluctuated. Some spots seemed to open suddenly, briefly exposing the inner depths of the sun.

A small dot, gradually swelling in size, held the attention of the Golden Amazon as she stared intently at the small viewing screen aligned with the protonic cannon. Sweat streamed down her forehead, gathering in little rivulets around the line of the dense purple goggles she wore to protect her eyes. Quickly she fingered the controls, centering the growing dot in the cross-hairs.

Across the control room, Abna sat again at the controls

only recently vacated by the Amazon, his hands flickering over the panels and keys like a master pianist. Sweat beaded his brow, as the air around them grew increasingly hot. The air conditioners whirred and clicked as they sucked in the heated air, cooled it, and re-circulated it in life-saving gusts. Abna moved a switch that dropped another purple shield over the windows. The sun no longer flared as a vast globe of blinding, incandescent flame, but as a sea of boiling flame, marred by the darker blotches of sunspots.

Like great clutching fiery tentacles, prominences reared upwards, seemingly deliberately reaching towards their ship, leaping half a million miles and more from the solar furnace below, then falling short as they were dragged back to the boiling surface by the mighty solar gravity.

"We're only a few million miles from the sun, Vi," Abna gasped from parched lips. "The gravity's got us good and hard, and our speed's increasingly rapidly. 80 percent of light speed, 82… Can you see Karg's vessel?"

"Yes, but we're still just out of range of this weapon. Increase speed, Abna!"

"That'll put us over the gravity demarcation line! At that speed we can't pull away from the sun! And," he added worriedly, glancing at the displays, "the outer hull is beginning to fuse!"

"To hell with that—increase our speed!" The Amazon snapped.

Grimly Abna obeyed, biting his lip as his fingers brushed against a metal panel on the control board. Instantly the contact caused an ugly burn.

"90 percent…93…"

"Now!" the Amazon exclaimed, and depressed the firing button. A battering, invisible stream of protons flashed towards Karg's vessel. It seemed to blossom like a speeded-up film of a flower, then flew apart and disappeared in a puff of incandescent gas.

"Got him!" the Amazon cried in triumph. "We—" her voice choked off abruptly as the temperature in the ship suddenly increased tremendously.

The Amazon and Abna had no time to work out what had happened as they felt themselves reeling into unconsciousness. Such was the speed of their ship, that they had, in fact, flown straight into the still-expanding fireball that was Karg's ship. The temperature of the exploded metals and gases was great enough to incinerate their ship within a second or two... But, such was their speed, that within microseconds, they were beyond that incandescent cloud of debris, and into clear space. Space that would not remain clear for long, however. At almost the speed of light they were hurtling straight for the rim of the sun. The leaping, hungry prominences came visibly nearer and nearer...

But now a tremendous strain gripped their ship. With the last vestiges of her expiring consciousness, the Amazon felt that something was plucking at every cell of her body. The very fabric of the universe rippled and tore—as first the Amazon and then Abna blacked out completely.

* * * *

Silence, eerie and complete.

The Golden Amazon groaned, and opened her eyes. She discovered that she was floating, face down, perhaps two feet from the metal floor. To one side, at the range of her vision, she could see the metal legs of the chair affixed to the floor in front of the controls for the protonic cannon. For a panicky moment, her mind was a complete blank. Then pain stabbed through her blistered hands as, twisting like an eel, she managed to reach out the fingers of her outstretched hand to grasp one of the still warm metal legs of the chair. She closed her eyes with the mild anguish, but at least the pain served to force her to full awareness.

Memory returned as she opened her eyes. She felt strangely weak. Her entire body ached with an intense burning itch, and she sensed that under her costume, her skin was covered with heat blisters. The emergency lighting, dim and almost yellow, was on. She realized at once that the ship was weightless, and they were traveling at a constant velocity.

Slowly she managed to punt herself to the switchboard. She pushed a button, and immediately crashed to the floor as the Earth-normal artificial gravity came into play. She lay there, stunned, for perhaps a full minute, wondering at her apparent weakness. Normally her super strong constitution should have found the short drop to the floor of little consequence. She staggered to her feet, holding on to the chair to assist her balance, and ignoring the pain in her hands as she did so. She glanced to the window.

The swirling gray mists of non-space confirmed her belief that the ship had entered hyperspace.

So they had escaped a fiery death in the sun—and Karg had been destroyed! Her next thought was for Abna. She turned. Abna was still in his seat, as he had buckled himself into it. He was slumped forward to a position of just a few inches above the narrow table skirting the bank of controls, his head resting on his left forearm, the other dangling at his side.

As she moved towards him, she tripped another switch that should have restored the main lighting, but nothing happened. Circuits probably burned out, she thought to herself. That brief fireball they had passed through—Karg's funeral pyre—had evidently caused some minor damage, at least.

Half fearfully, the Amazon reached out a blistered, tawny hand and felt for the great vein in Abna's massive throat. She sighed with relief as she felt a steady pulse.

"Abna!" she said, shaking him gently. "Wake up!"

"Vi… is that you?" Slowly Abna sat up, looking about him. He beheld the Amazon looking distastefully at the blisters on her hands, winced slightly as he became aware of his own identical condition. He smiled faintly.

"Well, as someone once said, 'Physician, heal thyself'…" He stared at his hands and concentrated.

As the Amazon watched, she saw the blisters and redness slowly ripple and disappear. Within seconds his skin was restored to normal. The Amazon raised an eyebrow and looked at him, without speaking. Abna smiled ruefully.

"Sorry, Vi. I needed to fix myself first, in order to better concentrate on fixing you up. Give me your hands."

The Amazon did so, gazing wonderingly into Abna's twinkling blue eyes. Although she had witnessed Abna's mastery of metaphysics on many past occasions, she never ceased to be amazed at his uncanny abilities. When she lowered her gaze, her hands and body had healed completely. Slowly she disengaged her fingers from Abna's gentle grip.

"Thanks," she said briefly. "I'll fix us a drink." She turned and went to a locker at the far side of the control room.

Abna smiled. Knowing the Amazon as he did, he had not expected more profuse thanks for the minor miracle he had performed. For the Amazon to have thanked him at all was phenomenal, and with that he was content.

When she returned with two glasses of restorative, she found Abna studying the instruments and displays intently.

"Our main lighting is out, and so are the refrigeration and air conditioning circuits," he announced, turning. "But that seems to be the extent of the damage. Should be easy enough to make the repairs." He reached out for the drink the Amazon held out to him. As he sipped it, he wrinkled his nose.

"It's warm," he complained.

"What else did you expect?" the Amazon said tartly. "Or have you forgotten that we've just flown within a few million miles of the sun?"

"Give me your drink, Vi." Abna held both glasses, staring at them intently. Then he handed the glass back to the Amazon. "Try it now," he invited.

The Amazon sipped, found it delightfully cool, and drained the glass. The drink held special food additives and restoratives that would aid their recovery.

Abna finished his drink also, and they put their glasses down on the base panel of the controls, which served as a table.

"That's better," the Amazon said. "I don't mind admitting that I felt as weak as a kitten when I woke up just now. Any idea how long we've been out?"

"According to the ship's chronometer, we've been travelling in hyperspace for four days," Abna responded. "And we'll go on doing so, unless we use the manual cut-out! Evidently you forgot to time-set the automatic controls, Vi!"

"I didn't forget," the Amazon bristled slightly. "There simply wasn't any need to do so. I didn't anticipate that we would be unconscious when we entered hyper space!" Then she shrugged, dismissing the matter.

"In four days," Abna mused, "we must have traveled one hell of a distance, relevant to our normal universe. We're deep into interstellar space. Better drop out of hyper pace now, Vi, so we can see where we are."

The Amazon nodded, and went across to the hyper-drive control unit. She studied the displays for a moment, then activated the manual cut-out. Again came that weird shimmering effect, a briefly painful plucking at the very atoms in their bodies, then they had returned to their own universe.

"We're still travelling at almost the speed of light," Abna remarked, his hands busy at the controls. Get back in your seat, Vi, whilst I slow us down. The deceleration will be pretty fierce, and may take some time."

At the end of five hours steady deceleration, Abna turned to the Amazon. "That's better, Vi. We're now down to a reasonable cruising speed, and can take stock of where we are."

The Amazon nodded and rose lithely from her seat. She strode over to the observation window and looked out.

For a long moment, she simply stared, without speaking. Abna, meanwhile, had removed a panel in the control board and was tinkering with a small soldering beam instrument. He gave a sigh of satisfaction as the yellow light was suddenly replaced by the normal more brilliant lighting.

"That's fixed the lights, Vi," he said. "Now for the air-conditioning—"

"Never mind that now!" the Amazon snapped. "Come

over here quickly! I—I don't think I've ever seen anything quite like this!"

Wonderingly, Abna came over and joined the Amazon in gazing out of the window into the region of space in which the ship had merged out of hyperspace.

They had emerged on the outskirts of an alien solar system. But the sight that met Abna's eyes clearly revealed that this was no ordinary solar system.

In fact, it was so bizarre that he was momentarily lost for words.

CHAPTER THREE

Deadly asteroid

In the depths of outer space, in the heart of the Milky Way Galaxy, a brief shimmering light suddenly appeared on the face of the deep, bright against the ebon darkness.

It quickly solidified into a shape like a silver shuttle—a spaceship from Earth, on board which were Viona, Mexone, and Thania. The automatic controls had performed flawlessly, controlled by the pre-programmed computer brains. After covering some two hundred light years—as measured in their own three-dimensional universe—the ship had cut its hyper drive engines and dropped back into normal space. It was now traveling at the same speed as it had been prior to the four-dimensional transition—a fraction below the speed of light.

Still the three Crusaders remained unconscious, as the forward rockets began firing, gradually slowing their terrific speed. They were thus spared the pain of the deceleration. Then—again with flawless timing—they received a restorative injection, and the rockets ceased as the ship gained a comfortable cruising speed, and a constant velocity.

Viona was the first to regain consciousness, and she lay for a moment as her strength returned as the restorative did its work. Like the others she had been in a state approximating suspended animation for almost five weeks. In the curved metal ceiling overhead, dim lights slowly increased in strength, even as did Viona herself.

Her glance swung to either side of her where Mexone and Thania were also rapidly recovering consciousness, lying on their pneumatic heavily sprung beds. Like Viona's, their bodies were gently straining against the bed straps. That meant that deceleration had ceased to pin them down. Their ship having achieved a constant velocity, everything in the vessel was weightless.

Viona released her straps, and expertly pushed herself to the switchboard. She pressed the button that restored the artificial gravity to permit of normal movement. Next she moved over to the observation port and gazed out into space upon the glittering backdrop of the Milky Way. A little sigh of satisfaction escaped her lips as she caught sight of a blazing star, ahead and just one side of them. Unlike the other stars around it, it was not a tiny point of light, but a distinctly discernible disk. Their target star!

So colossal was the distance to the region of interstellar space where the abandoned Ultra was drifting, that it would have been impossible to pre-determine the time spent in hyperspace so as to emerge into its immediate vicinity. Accordingly it had been decided to break the journey through hyperspace, and a 'target star' had been selected, as a first stage. Once they had materialized in this region, it would be possible to take fresh readings of the Ultra, and then to pinpoint its position more accurately. A second jump would accomplish their mission successfully.

"How are we doing, Viona?" The girl turned as Mexone came to her side, and slipped an affectionate arm about her shoulders.

"Excellently, from the look of things. I haven't had time yet to confirm our position from the instruments and computer readings, but that certainly looks like our target star up ahead. We're still on the outskirts of its solar system."

"If any," Mexone corrected. "We don't know yet if it has any planets. We're still too far away to observe them visually."

"I'll check it out," came Thania's eager voice behind and to one side of them, as she slid into the seat next to the telescopic and analyzing instruments panel.

Mexone shrugged. "You might as well, Thania. Give us something to do whilst we wait for the ship's computer to take fresh readings on the Ultra, and make the calculations for our final hop through hyperspace. That side of things is entirely automatic, so our involvement isn't needed, until it's completed. Then we'll make the final checks, and be off again into hyperspace—"

"Then we've also time for a proper meal as well," Viona decided, smiling. "After all, we haven't eaten any real food for the last five weeks. Help me prepare something, Mexone, whilst Thania is making her observations."

Mexone smiled to himself. As the newest member of the Crusaders, Thania still reveled in the thrill of discovering new worlds.

Over at the switchboard, Thania had set a delicate oscillating instrument in commission. She studied it with her merry gray eyes, scratched her head once or twice, then studied it again. Designed to pick up energy emanations, the instrument would immediately reveal the presence of any planetary body ahead in space… And it did.

As Viona, carrying a small tray, returned with Mexone,

Thania turned excitedly.

"Hey, you two—take a look at this!"

Smiling tolerantly, Mexone strolled over, and stooped to survey the pointer-needle. He gave a slight gasp, moved aside to let Viona look. It was hovering around an unheard-of energy vibration for space, far above that usually related to planets, or even asteroids.

"Amazing!" Viona declared, then as she studied it carefully she went on, "Do you two realize that this wavelength does not belong to inorganic matter at all? It has the wavelength one gets from organic matter—protoplasm, amoeba, and so forth. But what can there be of a protoplasmic nature in space itself? For that means… life!"

"That's just what I thought!" Thania declared excitedly. "If we continue on our course, we might find out exactly what."

Mexone hesitated, then shrugged. "Won't do any harm, I suppose. We still have a little time on our hands. I'd better take manual control though, and adjust our course a little. We're likely to skim past this system otherwise."

He returned to his seat at the switchboard, and adjusted the controls, increasing their speed slightly. The ship hurtled onwards steadily. On their respective screens, three pairs of eyes searched the void ahead, but they could not see any trace of the thing recording itself so infallibly on the detector… Space looked normal enough.

Away to the left as they traveled a planet was beginning to appear. Instruments revealed that it had a thick atmosphere, and in size appeared to be comparable to that of Venus. To the right were two large gas giants, many millions of miles distant, circling on the rim of this three-planet system. Mexone ignored them, and their retinues of small moons. Instead he set the course towards the smaller inner planet, orbiting perhaps thirty five million miles from its primary.

But this inner planet could not account for the extraordinary reading they were still getting, even though it lay in the same direction. Maybe the unknown was space-black and absorbed all light-waves…

After some two hours of steady progress Mexone frowned and rubbed his forehead. There was a pain in his brow, an unexpected one, as though his nerves had started to play hell with him. Queer! As a member of the superhuman Cosmic Crusaders his nerve was cast iron.

Then both Viona and Thania gave yelps of anguish, and twisted in their seats alongside Mexone. He turned a face that had a sudden drawn look.

"Something—is wrong with us!" he gulped. "I could swear my heart skipped a beat—or something—" He doubled up abruptly in a paroxysm, then when he straightened up again his cheeks were ash-white.

"Something is definitely attacking us!" Mexone panted, slumping back in his control chair and hugging himself. By this time both Viona and Thania were clearly little better, but being bigger he held on longer.

With the back of his hand he mopped his sweating face and stared out bewilderedly onto the void. Still nothing— But no! There *was* something, gray, impalpable—away to the left, perhaps five hundred miles distant, but so low in albedo it was hardly noticeable. Indeed it had probably escaped their earlier attention as a mass of cosmic dust or something. But it was there all right, giving off a queer pulsating glow.

Mexone twisted in his seat. "There! Take a look! Don't

you think that's what must be attacking us—?"

Anguished, Viona nodded weakly. "We're in no position to argue, Mexone. I feel like I'm dying! For God's sake, get us out of this—"

Mexone hesitated, then as he felt terrible pains burning into his mighty chest he swung the vessel around in a blaze of rocket jets and drove away as hard as the tubes would take him. And the greater the distance the less the Crusader's pain. At last they were normal again, with the ship coasting as Mexone cut the acceleration.

"What in cosmos was it?" Viona panted, color flowing back into her beautiful face. "It felt like a pair of forceps trying to pluck out my heart and nerves!"

"My sensations exactly," Mexone muttered bewilderedly.

"And remember that we only skirted it," Thania commented. "Definitely we have a job to do."

"A job?" Mexone asked, puzzled.

"A job for the Crusaders, I mean," Thania went on excitedly. "We know that the asteroid or whatever it is, is lethal to human life. Very well, we've got to find some way to neutralize it…"

"Viona?" Mexone turned to his wife. "What do you think?"

"I agree with Thania," the girl answered. "But this time we'll approach it again in heavy-duty protective suits…"

Mexone nodded and moved over to the storage lockers, dragged out three suits that looked rather like old-fashioned armor. The difference lay in the metal of which they were composed, which negated everything known in the way of radiation. Normally they were only used in a space emergency involving a dangerous level of radioactivity.

The three clambered into them, fastened up each others' square helmets; then looking like three robots they prepared for the return trip. Thania kept monitoring the detector, and Mexone once more took the controls. Viona was at the observation window.

Again they moved toward that gray smudge, watched it loom ever larger. But this time they felt none of the sufferings of the earlier visit. They could study the unknown at leisure, without pain, as they flew round it.

Its size was about that of a reasonably large asteroid. But from every position it appeared to be covered in the main by a grayish, mold-like substance.

"It looks like a rock gone bad," Viona commented through her helmet radio.

"Foul life," Mexone agreed, then turning to the instrument board he dropped a scoop attached to a wire from a trap in the ship's floor. Withdrawing a scoop full of the stuff he tipped it by mechanical means into a glass globe and sealed it quickly.

The Crusaders watched the curling, feathery reaction of the stuff against the inbuilt light in the globe. Certainly it was alive for it writhed incessantly.

"Bacteria?" Viona suggested.

"It has a similar formation," Mexone agreed. "But what sort of bacteria is it which can destroy over a distance— and in space? Guess we'd better try again," he decided, and once more the scoop dropped, this time bringing up samples of the basic rock itself under the sea of molds.

Carefully he stirred the gritty substance with a glass rod, whist the others watched intently.

"Dirt," Thania sniffed. "Nothing more. Bits of ice, that's all. All asteroids look alike anyway."

"They look alike, but they are not alike," Mexone corrected in a grave voice. "Asteroids, Thania, are messengers, telling us exactly where they've come from. From their makeup one can tell what part of the system they hail from: if not that, then the planet from which they have broken away…"

He got busy with the analyzing equipment, activating a device that sorted out the atomic weights and components of the stuff he'd obtained. Hardly any personal work at all was called for, for automatic and infallible computerized results were given. The pointer finally swung to the substance in closest parallel to it in composition in this system, drawing upon the data it had already stored following Thania's earlier observations of the various planets.

"The inner planet!" Mexone exclaimed, surprise showing behind his face glass. "This meteor came from there! That can't be right!"

"Instruments don't lie, Mexone." Viona looked back at the asteroid, puzzling for a while, then: "I'm beginning to get an idea about all this. We already know that the outer planets have several moons, whereas that inner planet does not."

"So what?"

"So what if that planet once had a moon? If it did, then at some point in the past it must have broken up: why, we do not know. The chances are that this chunk of moldy stuff is part of the one time inner planet's moon, which has drifted to this point of the system—by cosmic currents. How the life got onto it we do not know."

"Where does it get us?" Mexone asked. "We can't do much about a moon which vanished long ago."

Viona did not answer: she was busy with the instruments again, checking the drift of the asteroid carefully, working out details on the computer. When she turned to look at Mexone and Thania her face was worried behind the glass.

"It is drifting," she said slowly. "And it is slowly moving back into the inner planet's field. Within a very short time it will drop onto that world, and when it does, with those molds on it, God knows what will happen if that planet is inhabited!"

"As it probably is," Thania commented. "My earlier readings showed it to have a breathable atmosphere."

"So what do we do?" Mexone asked. "This ship doesn't carry any heavy armaments, remember. General Milford equipped the Amazon and Abna's ship with a protonic cannon for use against Karg, but our ship was not given any additional weaponry. All we have are standard heat rays. We might see if they can incinerate it."

"Yes—but if it is created by special action, incinerators will only destroy it temporarily, then it'll re-form. However, we can but try—"

Viona switched one of the heat beams into action and trained it on the asteroid. Smoky trails blasted through the fluffy, disgusting stuff and left deep scars upon it. But they formed again with miraculous speed.

"No use." Viona switched off impatiently, her eyes narrowing as the problem absorbed her. "It attacks over a distance and seems indestructible. Remarkable! And it is moving towards the inner world…"

"We've got to do something," Thania insisted. "Perhaps we could try crashing the ship into it at speed? Break it up with the impact?"

"Of little avail," Viona sighed despondently. "If we

broke it into small pieces the molds would still be upon it. That planet would get a rain of moldy meteors in various places instead of one huge lump—and the disease, or whatever it is, might wipe out its inhabitants. No; the better way is for us to fly on ahead and land on that planet. What we find there might provide the answer."

Mexone looked at her curiously. "What do you hope to find there?"

"Does it not strike you as possible that the inhabitants—if any—might have gotten rid of their moon on purpose because it was deadly to them? If it was anything like ours is, it was airless and dead: maybe it developed molds that were dangerous to that planet's life. So they blasted the moon out of the way—and bits of it swirled back to prove dangerous—like this asteroid… If the inhabitants did that they may know this time what it is and how to deal with it. So far that planet hasn't been properly examined. Now seems as good a time as any to get started. Only a theory—but worth following."

Thania nodded happily, ready for yet another possibly dangerous adventure. Mexone turned back to the controls, gradually pulled the ship away from the asteroid. Only then did they remove their stuffy suits. The small sample of mold by itself was powerless to do damage. Nonetheless Viona took the precaution of putting it in an open-topped culture jar. Later, it might be interesting to examine it at leisure…

CHAPTER FOUR

Mystery world

Working in shifts, Mexone, Viona and Thania hurtled their vessel across the void to the glowing planet, which lay dead ahead of them. In turn, they each watched it thoughtfully, wondering just what sort of a history it really had.

Their observations and readings pronounced it an ephemeral world—flowering gigantic verdure during the 720-hour day; and a mass of ice during the equally long night. A world that ran its seasons into a day's time. But of intelligent life and civilization they could not find any evidence.

The planet grew larger: the general mass of dense cloud was more distinct, blinding silver in the sunshine. Together now, the Crusaders watched the packed layers sweep up to meet them— Then they were in them, blanketed in dense mist, the total unknown on every side. Their speed was swift, so swift indeed they had left the daylit side of the planet before they realized it, were nosing blindly through murk, feeling their way. Eyes on the instruments, Mexone began to feel his way down. He realized instant destruction faced the ship if he cannoned into a mountain side or a glacier. Fortunately, the instruments revealed no such obstacles…

Lower—lower— Then with a bump that stopped the machine with a sudden crushing shock they landed. All was still—deathly still.

"Hmm—not so bright," Mexone murmured, peering into the abysmal dark. "Like a subway with the lights out."

But Viona was studying the instruments. "Air pressure a trifle denser than Earth's, but the mixture is the same. Nor is it so very cold down here on the surface—about twelve below zero. The frozen parts must be up at the atmosphere limit. Naturally the dense cloud will keep in the day warmth and make for slow dissipation—"

"I can see something!" Thania exclaimed suddenly, startled. "It looks like—a pair of headlamps!"

The others hurried over and stared outside. Not a thing was visible. The moonless, clouded night of the mystery world was absolute— Mexone was about to give a derisive snort when he saw there was something out there in the dark—two bright little spots! And they were moving! In time there were two more spots—then three more— Finally a dozen pairs of spots were in a semi-circle.

"Cats?" Viona volunteered.

"Or lights." Mexone frowned. "Don't think they can be lights, though, because they do not waver. We can soon find out…"

He depressed the exterior searchlight button and swung the controlling wheel. A blazing beam seared the misty dark outside and for a second or two the bright spots were framed in demoniac outlines. Scrawny little bodies, all head and pipestem neck, went scurrying into dead branches and undergrowth—to reappear again, watching from a distance.

"Natives," Mexone muttered. "Eyes like those of an animal, reflecting the lights of our ship's ports. So this planet has got life after all! Just confirms what we've found on all our space voyages—if life can evolve somewhere, it will…" He switched off and surveyed the dark. "We had better get a meal and then wait for the dawn. I don't relish tackling those things in the dark… In the meantime I'll fix a compass guide on the ship so we can trace it however far we may roam…"

They ate, they refreshed themselves, they waited. Then at long last pale gray began to filter through the density above. It increased very slowly…

Interested again, the trio moved to the window and surveyed once more. The queer beings of the night had gone now and the weary gray was throwing into relief a tangled wilderness of dry, sticklike vegetation, tall, bare trees; brown, iron-hard ground… But beyond all this was something else—smashed and eroded stone columns, Tumbled minarets, courtyards eaten to pieces by vines which hung dead at the moment…

Here undoubtedly lay the shattered remains of a once fine city. Now dead, ruined, desolate.

"As we came in to land, I'd formed the impression that this planet was a young and prehistoric world," Mexone said finally. "Instead it looks is though civilization has been and gone… Grab some tackle: we're going to look. Though I doubt if we'll find anything relating to that asteroid."

By the time they were ready it was full daylight—a blinding gray shade caused by the diffusion of piled-up cloudbanks. Outside, they found the hard ground had now deteriorated into a sea of sloppy mud in which green life frothed and burst. Ankle deep in it in their knee boots they moved along, packs on shoulders, flame-guns at their sides.

Every now and again they stopped, convinced of that uncanny feeling of being watched. Yet they saw nothing. Even so they felt sure a myriad eyes were watching their every move—a feeling lent added possibility by the shelter afforded now from vines and trees all sprouting into speedy life.

Then here and there on the stifling air came a chatter of laughter—the silliest laughter, like imbecile children.

"Uh-uh," Thania muttered uneasily, raising a sweating face.

"Definitely sinister," Mexone agreed, fingering his collar—but they went on just the same, but with increasing furtiveness. They were on a planet completely unexplored, and that might mean death at any moment.

In half an hour they reached the ruins of the city. Only their imaginations could tell them how immeasurably vast it must once have been. It stretched through the fast-growing vegetation for many square miles, parts of it still traced out. It could be pictured as thriving, industrious, devoid of all this vegetation now twining through its bones.

Buildings were without roofs; here and there walls stood in isolation, the tops crumbled. In other places machinery of no conceivable purpose lay rusted, abandoned, most of it out of shape from incessant exposure. Once, no doubt, science had held full sway here, and probably a high order of science at that.

Then presently, as the exploration was continued, the trio caught glimpses of that weird life of the night. Sometimes they saw a native hiding behind an eroded column; or at times a group of them looking over a hill of smashed machinery up which verdure traced its leisurely way.

"Like a bladder on a string," Thania said, as they glimpsed a native clearly for a moment.

"But their purpose?" Mexone muttered, his handsome face troubled. Instinctively he clutched his gun—and it was well he did so for as though with a prearranged signal a whole army of the creatures suddenly burst forth from a dozen hiding places, came speeding across the clearing.

They were queer all right—even hideous. Their bodies were only Earth-like in having trunk, head, arms, and legs. There all similarity ended. The bodies were like footballs with distended bellies. Legs and arms were scrawny, as were necks. The heads were top-heavily big and bald, supplied with two enormous eyes which obviously were intended to compensate for the pitchy night. Extraordinarily enough, each one of them wore an incredible ornament in addition to a rough loincloth. Sometimes the trinket was a radio-like component tied round the neck with vine; in other cases it was copper wire, green with age, made like a bracelet. Still others had metallic parts linked together in a waist girdle, and the parts were clearly from a dismantled machine!

So much the Crusaders had time to notice before they were overwhelmed. Mexone fired his gun and it blasted one of the beings to ashes—then he was flung over on his back for all his size, wriggled in nausea as he was pawed and gripped by hands as wet and cold as tripe.

He tried to fire his gun again, then cursed as it misfired. He jammed the gun back into its holster, and used his fists instead. Both Thania and Viona were attacked before they'd had a chance to draw their own weapons. There was tremendous strength in the skinny limbs—almost blind animal ferocity... For a few minutes Mexone and the two women gave back as good as they got, slamming their fists into cold, slippery flesh, injuring perhaps a dozen of the little horrors—but finally they won the day from sheer numbers, brought lengths of vine from the jungle and trussed the trio securely, laid them flat on their backs. They were tied in such a way that they were unable to exert their superhuman strength to the full. Despite the Crusaders straining desperately, the vines held them fast—for the moment at least.

A war dance began—anyway it looked like that if the peals of idiotic laughter and mad shouts were any guide.

Despite their personal danger, Viona looked back at the creatures with a vaguely scientific interest.

"Observe a few details," she said finally. "They're not animals. They have humanlike hands and feet—human appearance. They are not even highly evolved apes. I begin to think they are de-evolved from a more highly organized race."

"What gives you that idea?" Mexone grunted.

"The city. Some memory tie keeps them close to it. They are like jealous guardians. Maybe they thought we intended to desecrate it, or something."

Mexone didn't reply for the dancing and laughter had ceased. With a determined rush the creatures pushed forward, seized the trio in their pipe stem arms—it took six of them to raise Mexone—and began to carry them along. A journey into the jungle to places unknown began…

At the end of an hour of this the Crusaders were beyond comment. The creatures seemed to be pursuing an interminable journey: but finally it did come to an end as they began to break free from the matured masses of sweltering foliage and entered a clear, rocky space.

Here there was an extraordinary object upon which the Crusaders had time to gaze at leisure as they were tossed down.

The object was a squat, powerful affair of metal, somewhat weather worn, and looking rather like an inverted bottle. The neck section was rigidly fixed into a platform, this in turn being raised from the ground level by four short pillars… Beside it,like an immense cylinder, was a machine that defied analysis, particularly as its summit was fitted with an affair like a radio antenna.

Perhaps even more extraordinary was the fact that at this point—perhaps the only one on the planet—the sun was shining. To left and right of the clearing were titanic mountain ranges, but between them the clouds writhed and twisted incessantly, constantly thinning to permit one clear shaft of blazing sun to stream through. Like a pointing finger the ray settled exactly upon the queer machine on its platform. And round the contrivance the natives were dancing, their weird ornaments bobbing, their hands linked in each other's.

"At least it is clear what is happening in the clouds up there," Mexone commented at length. "There must be an eternal wind from the night side over the mountains, bringing a vast temperature change which mingles with the hot side. Result is the clouds up there rupture and sunshine gets through—"

"But why the dance?" Viona asked anxiously. "And what is that object anyway?"

"There, Viona, you have me— Hallo, here they come!"

Once again they were lifted, carried into that area of blazing sunlight. Their senses reeled for a moment at the impact of that orb, only thirty five million miles distant.

This sunlit area was like a furnace, and the glimpse they had of the sun was that of a liquid blue-white ball that gave them pink spots before their eyes for several minutes afterwards.

Drenched in sweat, agonized by the blaze, they were bounced and bumped along as the natives carried them round the platform base in dizzying circles, themselves apparently heedless of the blazing tide pouring down upon them.

Dazed and sick, Mexone watched the platform going round in apparent circles; then he noticed that underneath the platform was a deep pit, the underside of the platform raised from it by the four short pillars. He was trying to fathom its purpose when to his alarm he was suddenly hurled forward violently, sailed right into the pit and fell headlong.

He dropped some twenty feet into an evil-smelling, revolting dark. Then Viona fell on top of him, followed by Thania, jerking all the breath out of him… They all lay gasping and struggling for a moment, listening to the peals of idiotic laughter from above…

Then slowly, gradually, the laughter began to die away. A dead silence ensued.

"If you could get your teeth into these vines, Mexone," Viona said, we might be able to get out of this!"

Mexone stirred at the voice above him, at the heaving of his wife's lithe body, as she maneuvered her bound wrists towards his face. He shifted, obeyed the request, and some minutes later his strong teeth had partially chomped through the vine. Viona exerted her superhuman strength and the weakened vine snapped, freeing her wrists. From then on it was easy. Finally the Crusaders stood up, staring at the circular hole through which they'd dropped, and the base of the queer machine.

Thania gave a sudden sniff. "Hmm, it would seem the sanitation is pretty bad around here. Smells rather like a slaughter house."

It did. In fact the stench was appalling. The three of them began to move round to trace the cause of it, wondering if they had been tossed into a rubbish dump. Then Viona gave a sudden cry.

"Say, there's something here like the end of a dog's nose! Must be a native— Up you come!"

The others heard her gasp with effort and moved toward her. They found Viona supporting a native nearly too weak to stand. His huge eyes were visible, catching the light from above.

"I suppose," Viona reflected, "I ought to wring his neck? But seeing as we're in the soup together, I won't— Hallo, more of them!" she exclaimed, as getting accustomed to the gloom they could see three or four natives sprawled on the floor around them, apparently motionless—perhaps dead.

"Possibly they *are* dead," Mexone reflected. "That would account for the odor."

Viona nodded, shook the native she still held. "Is there any way out of here beyond climbing?"

The native responded with a chatter that meant nothing. Viona gave a despondent sigh. But Thania became active and went to the nearest wall, returning presently with the vine ropes they had cast off.

"Simple," she murmured complacently knotting them together—then tossing up the free end he let it fall around one of the pillars and so back to her.

"Being smallest," she said, "I'll go first."

Agilely as a monkey she went up, while Mexone and Viona watched her anxiously from below. Then as Thania motioned them to follow Mexone tossed the native over his shoulder. "You next, Viona."

Immediately she began to climb, emerged over the pit edge to find Thania looking about her with her raygun ready. Seconds later Mexone scrambled out, laying the native ahead of him on the rim of the pit as he emerged from below.

There was no sign of life. Apparently the natives had gone.

"Just wonder why they went to all that trouble?" Mexone asked, helping the native to his feet—then he gave a start of horrified surprise. Now the native was in daylight it was apparent his absurd body was covered with ugly sores.

"Uh-uh," Mexone said, inspecting himself. "Don't like the look of this—"

"Apparently burns," Viona pronounced, frowning. "Similar to those from X-rays. Not catching anyway, I fancy…" She turned to the native. "Tell me, do you understand what I am saying?" she asked.

The creature simply gazed with his catlike eyes. But there was an expression close to gratitude on his queer face. And at length he did try to explain himself, but in an impossible language.

"If only we could get him to talk sense we might be able to understand the set-up of this place," Viona sighed. "More than that, we might find something out about the asteroid. After all, that's our prime purpose."

"Pity we haven't got the language translator with us," Thania remarked. "But that's aboard the Ultra, light years away from here. Or," she added musingly, "if Abna were here he could mentally transfer our language—"

"That's it!" Viona cried. "That's what we're going to have to do. Mexone: you can help me. Let's get busy right away."

"Just what have you in mind, Viona?" Mexone asked, puzzled. "We don't have your father's metaphysical or mental powers."

"You don't, perhaps, but as my father's daughter I've inherited some small part of his powers—and Mother's too. And if you add your own concentration to mine, we might just manage it. His mind should be tractable, especially if I hypnotize him first..."

Thania looked on in silent amazement as Viona hypnotized the little man, a simple enough accomplishment. Then came the more difficult part, as Viona attempted to telepathically impress a knowledge of the English language, assisted by a furiously concentrating Mexone.

It was a feat that was regularly accomplished by Abna within a few minutes, but for Viona it was going to be a long, exhausting job—and it wasn't going to be made any easier by the thought of a mold-smothered asteroid creeping ever nearer to the planet.

CHAPTER FIVE

The Flying world

At length, Abna turned aside from the observation window and looked at the Amazon. "If ever a system warranted investigation, this one does! You agree, Vi?"

"Definitely. I'll get busy at the telescope," the Amazon said. "You check the instrument readings." Abna nodded and went across to the other side of the control room where the sophisticated radar and detection equipment was situated. Expertly he surveyed his instruments, activated switches.

The long range detector needle quivered into life. The moment any planetary or spatial body came within range, even though invisible to the eye, an alarm would ring and the detector, responding, would immediately fix the position of the disturbance.

Immediately the detector alarm awoke into noisy action. In an instant Abna was leaning over the instruments, keenly studying their reactions. He scarcely noticed that across the room the Amazon was seated at the telescope, her yellow fingers twirling the calibrated knobs and controls.

Without a word to each other they began to check and calculate carefully. The lenses of the detector came into use and visually picked up the cause of the distant alarm. When they had both gazed long and earnestly, Abna at his screen and the Amazon at the telescope, they straightened up and looked blankly at each other.

"Abna!" the Amazon exclaimed, startled. "That's the fastest planet I ever saw! Are you tracking it? It's flying round its Sun like a bullet!"

He puzzled silently for a moment, then operating the televisor screen he succeeded in bringing into even clearer focus on the screen the strange distant world of which the Amazon had spoken. Clear and distinct it was, a planet perhaps only slightly smaller than Earth, but behaving as no self-respecting planet should. Alone in its glory, apparently sheathed in ice, it was pursuing a highly eccentric orbit round its quite normal dwarf type Sun.

Starting from a close perihelion point it went sweeping out in a wild curve, zig-zagged sharply at one place on its route with a force that looked strong enough to tear it clean out of its path—then it pulled back again and went sailing at terrific speed to remote aphelion almost beyond visual range. A mad, silly little world obviously under the pull of gigantic gravitational fields—perhaps dead stars lurking unseen in the vast void. And as it went its surface coloring changed weirdly.

"It look to me, Abna," the Amazon said slowly, "that we've entered a binary system. That planet's eccentric orbit can only be explained if it is actually orbiting two suns! And one of them must be a dead star, because it's invisible—"

"It's more than that, Vi!" the Abna said decisively. "It's a black hole! The first we've ever encountered close up. And it *is* detectable on our instruments. Come and take a look…"

The Amazon came across and quickly slid into the seat vacated by Abna. "Look at these readings," he said quietly.

"You're right," she gasped. "Judging from the motion of the star we can see, and its planet, we can deduce the mass of the star we cannot see. It must be a massive star, perhaps eight to ten times the mass of our Sun! Normally such a star would be intensely bright—yet I couldn't detect any radiance from it in the telescope. It has to be a black hole, a collapsed star whose gravity is too massive for even light photons to escape."

"And it represents a massive danger to us," Abna remarked. "If we get too near it, we'll be sucked down into it, never to emerge! Get into your seat and strap in, Vi. I'm going to change our course, so that we'll keep well clear of it."

"Why not plot a course so that we'll intercept that planet when it makes its return trip to perihelion around the normal star?" the Amazon suggested. "That way we can land on it. If ever a planet warrants further investigation, it's that one!"

"What good would that do?" Abna objected. "You saw it through the telescope—the darn thing's frozen solid—"

"If you were more of a scientist and less of a dreamer we might do some useful work," the Amazon remarked tartly. "That world is only ice-sheathed at aphelion limit, which is when you looked at it. But when I observed it earlier, it became all green and gold at perihelion," she went on. "Sort—sort of chameleon planet," she finished wonderingly.

"Are you sure Vi? That coloring may just have been a spectrum warp in the lenses," Abna said dryly; but the

Amazon gave an angry snort.

"Spectrum warp be damned! Don't try and avoid the issue, Abna! That's a planet that may have something worthwhile on it, even if it does hold the cosmic speed record. We wanted relief from monotony—and we've got it! Get busy at that control panel and restore my faith in your scientific abilities."

Abna gave a wry smile. "I was only kidding, Vi. I'm already calculating the orbit we'll need to make a landing." Giving the power to the rocket tubes he swung the vessel in a gradual arc, reversing their line of flight—which, unchecked, would eventually have brought them to the dangerous vicinity of the black hole—and increased the smoothly cruising speed of the vessel to match that of the flying world. His maneuvers sent their spaceship plunging like a silver bullet through the cosmos while the Amazon, rigid over the instruments, rapped out instructions and suggestions.

True to calculation, the vessel came within close range of the flying world 120 minutes later, keeping pace with it in its hurtling journey.

Puzzled, the two looked down on its surface and watched the strange spreads of color that suffused it at varied points of its orbit. The nearer it came to the Sun the grayer it became, seemed to actually cover itself with clouds—then it moved on again at top speed, merging from gray to green, to blue, fading down into red, then white, and resolving at aphelion into primary black only barely distinguishable against the utter platinum-dust dark of space.

"Chameleon planet is right!" Abna breathed, fascinated. "I still don't see though what we'll find of interest on it. It's just a haywire rocket."

"Never mind talking about fireworks—descend and have a look at it!" the Amazon insisted. "Wait until it gets near the normal Sun and then drop down. At the rate it's going that will be at any moment..." Her eyes followed it speculatively as it raced away into space.

Abna bent more closely over his controls, easing the vessel sideways from the planet's gravitational pull. With tensed muscles he waited. His gaze, along with the girl's, followed every movement of that hurtling globe as it suddenly began its return trip.

He gripped the major control switches tightly and began to jockey the vessel round, twisting it in a great arc and then flattening out as the racehorse planet tore past.

His judgment was superb—the space machine leveled out at 1,000 feet above the gray, turbulent surface. Working dexterously he drove the nose downwards, plunged into the midst of the gray and found to his satisfaction that it was cloud, cushioning atmosphere that broke the terrific down rush of the ship and eased her gently to a surface that was spongy and steaming with amazing warmth.

The vessel dropped softly at last in the center of a small clearing, surrounded by immense trees. They rose on every hand in fantastic array, their lower boles as smooth as billiard balls and bluish gray in color. Beyond this shiny, bald space they sprouted into circular tiers of similar hue, oddly like hundreds of umbrellas piled on top of each other.

Even as the startled two looked at them through the window they visibly grew and added fresh veined vegetation domes to their height, quivered in the mystic ecstasy of some inner life. Nor were they isolated in their queerness... In the midst of the lush soil, vines of vivid green twirled their roots and tendrils in and out of stolid looking bellying bushes like gargantuan mushrooms. Everywhere, in every direction, was a swelling, tangling wilderness of stubbed, crazy shapes—here bulging, there elongating, like the irrelevant, frightening illusions of a nightmare.

"Life—gone mad!" murmured Abna soberly, then he turned away and glanced at the external meters. He felt vaguely satisfied at finding an atmosphere compatible with Earth's, a gravity almost identical, but a temperature and humidity equaling that of the Carboniferous Age.

"Breathable, but as hot as hell," the Amazon said expressively, gazing over his shoulder. "We could still go outside without helmets, though: the sun's clouded so I guess we can risk it."

Abna glanced again at the fantastical, swaying life, then he gave the Amazon a dubious look.

"It's a risk," he said. "I don't mean the air—I mean the form of life out there."

"Are we Crusaders or not?" the Amazon retorted. "I didn't think you were the sort of man to get cold feet now! If you won't go, I will. That's flat!"

Abna caught the challenge in her flashing violet eyes. He nodded a trifle reluctantly.

"O.K. we'll chance it, if only to grab a few specimens. But we'll take full precautions, though. Fit up backpacks with complete space suits as well as provisions. Use the space-bags; they'll stand any conditions. I'll contrive a portable tent and select some suitable defensive weapons."

"Check!" the Amazon nodded eagerly, her scientific soul alight to the challenge of a new and unknown world.

* * * *

Five minutes later, surrounded by surging waves of sickly greenhouse warmth, they were standing together just outside the ship, the airlock securely fastened behind them. Their backs were loaded with full pack, Abna bearing the larger accoutrement in the form of a strong but collapsible thin metal tent.

In silent dubiousness they looked around them on the umbrella trees and tangled shooting life that sprouted with insane fervor on every hand. Despite the heavy, drifting clouds they could feel the intense heat of the Sun beating down on their heads, its ultra violet radiations tingling the skin of their bare arms. They began to perspire freely.

"Well, Vi, what's your suggestion?" Abna asked querulously. "Looks to me as if just wandering in this tangle will make us perform a complete vanishing trick."

"We're explorers, not magicians," the Amazon answered briefly. "We can at least grab a few of these plants for specimens. Let's go!"

She stepped forward boldly, flame pistol firmly gripped in her hand.

Abna looked after her lithe, slim figure for a moment, then with a resigned shrug prepared to follow her. Mentally he decided that the whole excursion was more risky than the Amazon seemed to think… He moved, like the girl, with studied care, glancing around and below him at the twisting vines and sprouting shave-grass. Here and there in the patches of damp loam there frothed areas infested with minute, scuttling life, and, for every step he took, he had to dodge aside to avoid a wickedly spired carmine-hued stem as it rose like a livid bayonet from alluvial soil.

So intent was he in guarding himself, indeed—in surveying the ground, he momentarily forgot the girl, until a sudden wild shout from ahead caused him to look up with a start.

Horrified and amazed he came to an abrupt halt. The Amazon was rising upwards into the air in front of the nearest umbrella tree, the carmine stem of a bayonet-bamboo thrust through the tough leather belt about her waist! Struggling wildly, she reared up to a height of thirty feet, striving frantically to free herself and calling his name.

The ludicrous figure she cut made Abna smile for a moment—then with a single slash from his flame gun he cut the plant in two and broke the girl's fall as she came toppling down helplessly into his arms.

"We've no time to play at acrobats," he reproved her dryly, as she straightened her rumpled clothing. "You ought to know better, Vi."

"Could I help it if the thing grew while I was studying an umbrella tree?" she demanded wrathfully. "This place is so darned swift you need a time machine to keep up with it! The speed of the growth of these things around us is utterly unexpected. I think we should go back to the ship the ship before worse things happen!"

She broke off as she half turned. Dismay settled on her beautiful face at the sight of spreading, spiraling masses of incredible growth. In the few brief minutes occupied in her bayonet-stem adventure the clearing had changed utterly.

Wild, rampant growth had sprouted up soundlessly on all sides, had already hidden the ship from view. Colors, weird and flamboyant, provided a crisscrossing maze of bewildering interlacings. Umbrella trees, bayonet-bamboos, bile-green vines, swelling objects like puff balls— they were all there, creaking in the hot, heavy air with the very speed of their growth, providing a blur of vivid colors that was eye-aching.

Abna did not need to be told that the ship was fast being smothered. The Amazon's sudden startled silence was sufficient. For a moment he was nonplussed, then gripping her by the arm he plunged forward towards the tangled mass with flame gun spouting in a vicious arc, but even before he had the chance of seeing what happened an intense, saturating darkness flooded down.

"Now what?" he snapped in exasperation. "Have I darn well gone blind or—"

"No, Abna—it's night!" The Amazon's voice was wondering as her hand gripped his arm. "At the terrific speed this planet rotates and moves the day's already exhausted! We'll have to try— Ouch!"

She broke off and staggered in the darkness as a vicious unseen thorn stabbed the bare flesh of her arm. Abna drew her more tightly to him and switched on his belt torch. The clear beam revealed the solid, impregnable mass on every side.

Bewildered, they stumbled round, all sense of direction confused. Razor-edged masses were springing up now, mercilessly sharp, leaving slashes on their tough leather knee boots... Gripping each other they moved onwards, literally forced to do so to escape the mad life twirling insanely around them.

Twice they blundered into an umbrella tree, reeling aside only just in time to escape the sudden sharp closing of its upper folds. It seemed to be more a mystic reflex action than actual carnivorous strain.

At last the girl halted as they came into a slightly quieter region.

"Look here, Abna, what are we going to do?" she panted. "In case you don't know it we're completely lost!"

He stared at her torch-illuminated face. "I'm open to suggestions, Vi," he said frankly. "We can't find the ship again in this stuff, that's a certainty. We have provisions to last maybe a month, and in that time—"

"A month!" she echoed, moving quickly as she felt an avid vine shooting over her feet. "How do you figure we're going to survive a month in this hole? We'll be stabbed or strangled long before that!"

"Wonder what causes it? The growth speed, I mean." Abna's voice came musingly out of the dark. "Incredibly fast plant mutations must have some cause behind them. Maybe something to do with the planet's orbital speed. Even time seems different here. From space this world looked to be revolving like a humming top, yet now we're on it night and day seem to arrive normally—"

He stopped short as at that identical moment the stifling, terrible dark suddenly vanished and gave place to daylight again. The glare of the cloud shielded Sun flooded down on the wild growth, which, in the case of the umbrella trees at least, had already achieved cloud-scraping proportions.

"Normal, eh?" the Amazon questioned laconically, but she was obviously relieved.

"Well, if not normal, it at least resembles day and night," Abna amended. "I expected something so swift that we'd encounter a sort of winking effect."

The Amazon said nothing to that; her eyes were traveling anxiously round the confusion. The thought of the vanished space ship, the absolute craziness of everything, was obsessing her mind.

"Only thing to do is to keep on going," Abna decided at length. "Maybe we'll find a place to pitch camp and lay further plans."

"I wish I shared your optimism," the Amazon sighed, then gave a shrug. Easing the burden of her pack she prepared to follow him...

Forced to keep moving by reason of circumstances the two blasted their way with flame guns through the crazy rampancy ahead of them. Confused, bewildered, they found themselves constantly confronted with things defying understanding.

One particularly vicious type of plant, which they nicknamed the 'bellow bulb,' caused them a good deal of trouble. Lying in the soggy soil like a bladder, it released a powerful lethal gas when trodden on. More than once they found themselves tottering away from these things on the verge of unconsciousness.

But at last they became thankfully aware of the fact that the insane growth of the jungle was ceasing. The vast agglomeration of trees and plants seemed to have reached maximum size: there was no longer danger from slicing barbs, blades and thorns... Once they realized a passive state had been achieved they sank down gratefully on one of the ground-level vines and took their first nourishment.

"Wish I could figure it out!" Abna muttered worriedly, twirling a tabloid round his tongue. "In all our explorations throughout the universe, we've never encountered a planet like this one."

"Looks to me as though this is a sort of swamp age," the girl muttered, thinking. "Look around you: the plants have stopped growing, By all normal laws they ought to start collapsing to form future coal— Oh, but what am I saying!" she exclaimed hopelessly. "It simply isn't possible for that to happen so that we could see it. The formation and creation of coal is the work of ages."

"I'm not so sure of that, Vi. On a normal world it is, certainly—but here we have a world opposed to normal," Abna pointed out. "Since orbital speed is so swift it is possible that evolution might be the same way. Remember that the plants taken to the moon by lunar colonists eventually mutated so that they pass through their whole existence in the span of a lunar month. On Earth a similar occurrence would demand a much longer time. On this chameleon-like planet anything might happen…"

"Might!" the girl echoed. "It *does*!"

"I wonder," Abna mused, "if the explanation for all this is somehow bound up in this planet's proximity to the black hole?" Abna fell silent, vaguely perplexed, then he aroused himself to speak again.

"Guess we might as well pitch camp here for the time being," he said briefly. "We need rest before we think out the return trip—granting there'll ever be any! Give me a hand."

The Amazon came willingly to his assistance as he slid the portable shelter from his back. In the space of a few minutes the ingenious contrivance with its hinges, brackets and angles was snapped into position, its slotted little beds sliding into fixtures as the four walls were clamped.

Grateful for the protection from the fierce ultra violet radiations of the clouded Sun, the two scrambled inside and pulled off their provision packs; then for a while they sat together on the edge of the beds, gazing through the open doorway… until Abna stiffened abruptly as his keen blue eyes detected a slight movement in the nearby undergrowth. Instantly his hand went to the flame pistol in his belt.

"What—what is it?" breathed the Amazon in amazement, gazing with him as there emerged into view a remarkable object like a monstrous earwig, two bone encrusted eyes watching from the midst of a rat-like face.

"Outsize insect," Abna said quickly. "Harmless, I guess."

He lowered his gun and waited tensely, in increasing amazement, as between shave-grass and creeping-plants huge creatures like salamanders pulled themselves into sight, their queer three-eyed, crescent shaped skulls giving the effect of Satanic grimace.

Next came creatures akin to scorpions, armed with viciously poisoned needles that quivered like daggers on protruding whip-like tails. Insects began to flit about—titanophasmes, as big as eagles. Above the tops of the lower lying liana alien dragonflies with yard-wide wings streaked swiftly… Nor was that all. There were immense grass-hoppers, millipedes as big as pumpkins, nauseous spiders dangling on ropy threads… A hideous and incredible vision.

The two Crusaders sat for perhaps fifteen minutes anxiously studying the creatures, when night fell again with its former startling suddenness. Day had lasted exactly two hours!

Abna gently closed the door and switched on his torch. It's light revealed that the Amazon's face was strained—not with fear, but with sheer bafflement.

"Two hours day; two hours night," she said wonderingly. "This place is absolutely crazy, Abna! And as for those phantasmagoric things outside! You're not suggesting we stop here with them around, are you?"

"What else do you propose, Vi?" he asked quietly. "We daren't go outside—we'd be worse off than ever. No; the only thing to do is to stick it and hope for the best, hard though it is."

Despite her lack of fear the Amazon shuddered a little. "Probably you're right, but it's not going to be easy."

She relapsed into silence. After a time Abna opened the door again and risked using his flashlight to see exactly what was transpiring outside. To the utter surprise of both of them the jungle was collapsing! The entire mad growth was breaking up into dried sticks and dust....

And the insects! They scuttled round in the confusion, yet not for a moment did they look the same. By lightning changes they increased in size, lost their insectile appearance and became sheathed in scaly armor. The stupendous dragon-fly creatures whizzing overhead grew larger with the moments, also achieved a protective covering that pointed beyond doubt to a reptilian strain...

At length finally, by the time daylight arrived once more, a new metamorphosis was complete. The two gazed out in awe on a scene magically different—evolution had slid by in a brief two-hour night! Another jungle was rising, but of a more delicate, refined nature, from the ruins of the old. Ferns of considerable size had sprouted in the clearing—behind them in fast growing banks were gently waving masses bearing strong resemblance to earthly cycads and conifers.

But nowhere was there a flower: only the fantastically colored vegetation held back from crazy growth by some new mutational law in the planet's inexplicable chemistry.

"If we set back for the spaceship now we might just find it," the Amazon remarked. "The going would be simpler, anyhow. What do you think?"

"So far as the jungle is concerned, yes," Abna agreed;

"but there are other perils. Look over there!"

He nodded his head to the opposite side of the clearing and the girl recoiled a little as she beheld a vast head of gray, the face imbecilic in expression, waving up and down on the end of a long neck. Flexible, rubbery lips writhed in avid satisfaction as the extraordinary beast lazily ate the soft, fast growing leaves of the smaller trees. Once, as the wind parted the vegetation for a moment, there was a vision of vast body and tail.

"Why, it's—it's an iguanodon!" she cried in horror, but Abna shook his head.

"Not exactly it, but very much like it. Herbivorous, of course… You know, Vi, it's just beginning to dawn on me what's wrong with this planet—why life on it is so crazy."

"Well, although I'm glad to hear the scientific side of your brain has finally started to function, I'm still anxious to get back to the ship," the Amazon said worriedly. "We can risk the monsters. That herb-eater is harmless enough, anyhow."

"But it won't be the only type," Abna reminded her grimly. "There'll be all kinds of things abroad—perhaps as frightful as our own one-time diplodocus and allosaurus."

"You mean we just stop here?" The Amazon's eyes were on the gray head. The swarming plant life had now almost hidden it.

"Until human life comes, anyhow," Abna said reflectively.

At that the girl twisted round from the doorway and stared at him amazedly.

"Human life!" she echoed. "Are you crazy! If you think I'm going to sit here while these playboys grow up through millions of years you're mistaken! I'm heading back right now for the ship!"

"In what direction?" Abna asked dryly, and the Amazon pursed her lips.

"I'll find it!" Her tone was defiant. "I've got a wrist compass just the same as you have!"

Abna shrugged and leaned more comfortably against the doorway. For a while he heard the determined bustling movements of the Amazon behind him—then her activity slowed down a little. At length he found her beside him.

"Maybe you're right, Abna," she admitted, with a rueful smile. "But at least you might tell me what you're getting at."

"It's simple enough. Evolution on this world is straightforward, fast though it is. The only way it differs is in that it passes through it mutations all at one sweep of existence instead of dying and being born again, in a more adaptive style. The giant creatures of this moment are the very same insects and millipedes we saw last night—same minds, only changed outwardly by an amazing mutational process. Just how this is possible we don't yet understand, but undoubtedly that black hole is at the back of it."

"I think you're right," the Amazon mused. "We know how black holes are created. After stars suffer a collapse so powerful that no known nuclear force can prevent it, they create a warp in the fabric of space time—and disappear into it, becoming what we call black holes, for want of a better expression. We don't understand the physics of black holes, but we can conjecture that they might be apertures to an entirely separate universe, where our laws of space and time do not apply."

"Exactly, Vi. Once captured, nothing from our universe can ever escape from them. But isn't it possible that forces from the *other* side might seep into our universe and affect time in its vicinity? Since this planet has such a weird orbit that causes it to skirt the black hole, it probably accounts for it. Its close approach to the Sun at perihelion produces Carboniferous Age conditions: as it recedes further away the condition will cool to normal, finally reaching a frozen glacial state compatible only with Earth's last days. What I'm wondering is, what will happen when we reach that zig-zag part in this planet's orbit, when it skirts the black hole. May be trouble."

The girl puzzled for a moment. "I do believe your mutational idea is dead right, Abna. What became of the First Glacial Epoch, though? That should have appeared between the insect and mammalian stages."

Abna shrugged. "Because it happened on Earth doesn't say it must happen here. In fact it's wholly unlikely. Life here will simply progress from warmth to cold, and during that period we'll have a pretty good simile of the lines Earthly evolution will take. This planet being practically the same in mass and atmosphere it isn't unusual that similar life to Earth's should evolve."

The Amazon looked out over the changing forest, her brows knitted. For an instant her gaze caught the gray hurtling form of monstrous archaeopteryx—a natural helicopter.

"Evolution like that still seems so impossible," she muttered.

"Why?" Abna objected. "On the contrary it's very sensible. Death, and thereby a possible break in the continuity of knowledge, is done away with. Besides there is a biological parallel to bear it all out."

"Meaning what? Surely you don't mean Haeckel's Recapitulation Hypothesis?"

"That's exactly what I do mean! Haeckel pointed out long ago that a human embryo before it is born undergoes in nine months all the primeval states. The fertilized egg form from which the human biped develops is, in the first instance, a primeval amoeba. In the nine months of its genesis it performs, unseen except by X-ray, the very incredible fast evolution we see here in actual fact. First the amoeba cell, the clustered cells like a mulberry—a globular animalcule. It then moves on to the fish stage and shows visible gills: it traverse the scale of the lower invertebrates. Fishes, amphibians, reptiles, lower mammals, semi-apes, human apes, and lastly *homo sapiens* are all passed through. Then the child is born. If it can happen invisibly to a human embryo, why not here in the form we behold? Maybe it is the only way Nature can operate. Being pressed for time, as it were."

"But all those recapitulations of other ancestral life forms are only *resemblances*," the Amazon objected. "And only the *earliest* forms of each, not the later complete animal."

"Of course they are," Abna agreed. "But that is on Earth. Here, on this alien planet of a black hole, we have the complete physical manifestation."

The Amazon continued to frown for a moment, then gave a shrug. "I suppose you're right. Certainly your theory appears to fit the facts. Then you think then that man will appear in, say, two days?" she questioned thoughtfully.

"Not quite so soon, perhaps, but certainly before very long. It may represent inconceivably long generations to this life but we measure time by the hours on our watches. The ship won't hurt in the interval. It's safely locked anyhow. When this forest dies down to give place to new forms we'll be able to find it easily enough."

The Amazon nodded agreement and settled herself down again to await developments.

CHAPTER SIX

Destroyer from the past

Impressing a knowledge of the English language into the brain of the native was more difficult than Viona had imagined. Because she did not possess anything like her father's mental capabilities, she found it exhausting. However, she and Mexone slogged doggedly on because it was the only line of action. Two Earth days elapsed, but there was no sign of returning natives. Food and drink was not a problem, because of the supplies they had brought with them in their packs.

Now and again Mexone took a turn with the 'education,' and gradually between them, they began to get results. Besides, they rather liked the little native in spite of his skin trouble. He was quite obviously intelligent—and still grateful. And at last, to the infinite relief of the two, he got to the stage where he could put words together to make sentences.

"Would—like to thank you—for food and water," was his opening statement. "And for rescuing me from down there. Would have died like fellows otherwise. Was thrown there because of this—" and he pointed to the burned looking patches on his body.

"What are they?" Mexone questioned sharply.

The native pointed to the sun, said simply. "Certain rays."

"I imagine," Viona said thoughtfully, "that certain radiations of the sun, in excess, have gotten him into this mess. Just the same as overzealous sun-bathers get ulceration."

"Name of me is—Vilji," the little man volunteered.

Mexone said paternally, "Vilji, we seek information. What race do you belong to? What are you all doing here?"

That took Vilji some time to explain and demanded pantomime, but from his mixed up metaphors and split infinitives it finally became fairly clear that the name of this world was Nuz, and he and his race were descendants of the original scientists who had built the now eroded city.

"We remember them little," Vilji sighed. "Once there was greatness, but we know it only from records. Space travel was tried: the man who tried crashed on our moon. His body fell prey to a metallic life on that moon. A new sort of life so came into being—a mold-like life. It needed living people like us so it could live. It formed into a fog, came down to our planet here, and killed many thousands, leaving weak survivors. Our scientists built a gun to destroy that moon..." And the pipestem arm indicated the queer 'inverted bottle' on its platform.

"I was right," Viona breathed. "Degenerate survivors. They have only memories, and a hereditary instinct keeps them still near to the city where there was once such pomp and power..."

"And the origin of that mold life is now explained," Mexone said slowly. "And a pretty incredible story it is. An alien life form that was completely transformed when it encountered and absorbed the life-force of that space explorer. It grew and expanded, eager for fresh life-force, to grow into something that threatened this world…"

"And after the moon was destroyed," Viona put in, "the mold went into a state of suspended animation, true to its bacilli-like qualities. When our spaceship approached it, with three superhumans aboard, it was like a feast for it! It absorbed our life energy, revived itself enormously."

"Exactly," Mexone agreed soberly. "Had we not left the area as quickly as we did, we would all have died—sucked dry of our life-energy. As it was our constitutions are such that we were able to recover fairly quickly." He turned and gripped the Nuzian by his shoulder. "Just what did they use in that gun to destroy a moon?" he asked urgently.

Vilji reflected, then said brightly, "Split power."

Viona frowned then gave a broad smile. "Split atoms—atomic force! Of course!"

She paused as the Nuzian apparently made up his mind on some objective, motioned them to follow him. They hesitated, wondering if it was a trick. Then Mexone gave a grunt.

"Might as well go with him. I think he is genuinely grateful for being dug out of that drain. We could do with new scenery."

They accompanied him through the riot of jungle until he came to a tiny clearing. Without hesitation he went on his knees and burrowed in the ground, finally dragged to view a roughly made box of tree bark. With all the reverence of finding a treasure he handed it over, a look of sublime trustfulness on his face.

Mexone took it solemnly, to find Viona smiling regretfully. "Sad," she said, "to think of a mighty race reduced to burying things like dogs! What's in it? Bones?"

Mexone jerked up the lid and stared in surprise at the

odd assortment. It was rather like the junk a child might collect—many trinkets, odd bits of wood and metal, coils of wire— And finally a sheaf of stiff parchment paper on a drum, to which was affixed a handle.

"More of the trinkets these Nuzians all wear as ornaments," Mexone mused. "Remains of scientific apparatus, I'd say. Obviously they have plundered the city's remains. But this parchment drum looks more interesting…"

Mexone examined it thoughtfully, turning the handle. The sheets instantly whirred and he gave a violent start.

"For you," Vilji offered. "Special treasure—of mine."

"Special treasure's right!" Mexone breathed. "Look here—! This darn thing, if Vilji only knew it, is movie history. It's one of those things where a selection of photographs, each advanced in action, gives a moving picture impression— Lord, if only we had all of it! Even as it is it's enough… See!"

The Crusaders watched, fascinated. As the handle turned the sheets flickered into a blurry movie of a city by moonlight—obviously this same city that now lay in ruins—for a good distance from it was a half completed device, unmistakable in shape. That atomic gun!

In the moonlit streets of the city lay thousands of dead, or slowly moving Nuzians, most of them struggling and milling away from the tentacles of a deadly fog reaching down from that moon.

Unhappily there was not much of the record, but it was enough to plunge the Crusaders into thought for a long time after they'd run it through several times. Finally Mexone summed up.

"We know the molds started by an alien metallic element absorbing the life of a Nuzian space explorer. It needed more organic life to keep it going—so it bridged the gap here to Nuz. When that happened the gun was only half finished. Obviously there was time to complete it. It blasted that moon into bits, hurling the parts to all quarters of the system. The mold-like stuff no doubt went into a form of suspended animation, came to life again on one of the floating pieces when it realized powerful life—inside our spaceship—was near it. It absorbed our life-force over a distance and grew in consequence. If it hits Nuz it will consume all life."

"But," Viona interjected, "we also know from this record that the gun was built in sections—plate by plate. And it used atomic force."

"I don't see the connection," Thania was puzzled.

"If it blew a large sized moon into pieces it could reduce an asteroid to dust," Viona pointed out. "It might even be capable of destroying that mold-life completely."

"But how in heaven's name do you propose to get a gun that size into space?" Thania asked.

Viona smiled. "It is in sections! If we could dismantle it—!" She turned to the Nuzian. "Tell me, Vilji, do you know anything of the art of gun dismantling?"

That was a teaser—but put in more simple language the Nuzian began to ponder. Finally he led the way back to the gun-site and the two watched him as he climbed onto the platform. Exerting but little effort he pushed on one of the gun's curved plates— Amazingly enough it came away along grooves and dropped with a clang, exposing the gun's interior.

"Of course—a portable gun!" Mexone cried. "This site is much further away from the city than the one in the movie record. The thing can be moved— How very, very interesting! Come!"

They climbed up to the Nuzian's side and peered through the opening into the firing chamber of the thing. It was complicated beyond belief, but all housed in weatherproof casing. This, and its superb workmanship, had effectually defied the ages.

"Atomic all right," Viona said finally. "See, here are the firing electrodes—and here's the matrix in between. Then the power is concentrated here. But look, what would they fire? Shells?"

"Through a portable gun?" Mexone shook his head emphatically. "No; they wouldn't need to fire anything—only the ray or beam of force generated by atomic disruption. Probably they used copper blocks in the matrix and the resultant energy was trained upward. Come to think of it we have copper aboard our ship which might come in useful."

They turned aside and looked further, discovered how easy a thing it really was to take to pieces. The bore itself was not in the least reinforced, proving beyond doubt it was only made to direct a force beam and not a shell… That settled it. They went to work taking away plate after plate, piling them up into a small hill on the platform. Then when they'd gotten right down to the matrix itself Mexone gave a groan of dismay.

"We have no power to fire it!"

"Not so!" Vilji insisted, who had been watching the proceedings with interest. Indeed, he seemed to have grasped the scientific implications completely for he pointed to the odd-looking cylinder with the 'radio antenna' on top of it. He made a motion to show it was dangerous, then pointed to the sunshine streaming onto it.

Finally he pressed a switch low down near the base.

The result was amazing. The cylinder hummed violently and the electrodes at each side of the gun matrix began to glow. Invisible disruptive radiations collided with one another since there was nothing in between to be disintegrated.

A recoil of hot air and choking dust all but pitched all of them off the platform. Instantly the Nuzian struggled over to the cylinder and switched off. Then he motioned to its various wires. Some led to the gun-matrix, and others sank into the ground.

"I think I understand," Mexone said slowly. "They erected the cylinder just here because of the eternal sunshine. It must absorb solar power and store it up as potential. And the earth wires take care of the surplus charge… And from the look of it the cylinder can be moved too. Well, we have the power—and the gun. I see the destruction of that asteroid coming much nearer!"

"How about getting this equipment out of here?" Thania asked.

"You must go and fetch the ship. And hurry! Viona and I will do our best to get this firing cylinder detached."

Thania nodded, vaulted to the ground, studied her compass for the way back to the ship, then hurried off with leveled ray gun. Mexone and Viona watched him out of sight, then turned back to the job…

* * * *

They had just gotten the cylinder free when a sudden hullabaloo arrested their attention. The Nuzians were returning, their shouts and yells filling the air. And this time they were armed with weapons—deadly looking things like ray guns, only smaller. Mexone gave a start of alarm as the rays from one of them chipped metal clean out of the platform. Immediately he drew his own reloaded gun, shot an anxious look at Vilji.

"They furious," he explained. "This gun—sacred shrine to them— Don't know real meaning of it. Not scientist like me."

"Act of desecration, eh?" Mexone's face went grim. "Okay; but we're carrying on just the same—" and he lashed round his gun suddenly. Two Nuziians dropped in clouds of ash.

Mexone ducked, dragged Viona and Vilji down with him. The frightful force of the ill-aimed Nuzian weapons was tearing chunks out of the platform, and less frequently the apparatus. Mexone's anxious eyes wandered to the cylinder of potential force. If there was a direct hit on that he didn't dare imagine what might happen.

"I suppose they've frisked these guns from some arsenal in the city?" he asked.

Vilji nodded worriedly. "That is why they have been quiet. They went to get them. Atomic force. Like big gun here."

"Which means they have an almost infinite supply of power," Viona sighed. "Nice going!"

She dodged again as more ray charges flashed around her. She took careful um, peering round the mass of the dismantled gun. Another wildly charging Nuzian went down with half his body blown away.

Both Mexone and Viona were troubled. There was something nauseating about all this. They'd sooner have a good clean fight with flesh and blood than a lot of *papier maché* beings like this. And the fact that they were trying to save them from a horrible doom—had the Nuzians but known it—added a bitter irony to the proceedings.

Whang! They flattened as a chunk of metal cleaved out, V-shaped, immediately over their heads. Another charge flashed violently on the precious gun matrix—but nothing happened. Mexone breathed again. No damage done apparently, except for the smoky mark on the casing…

After awhile, to his deepening horror, the Nuzians began to close in more obstinately, reinforced by greater numbers from behind. All of them it was clear were hell bent on destroying the machinery and the defilers with it.

Time and again Mexone and Viona fired at them vigorously, but in any case they had not enough gun-charges to account for all of them— So first one gun and then the other finally ran out and they tossed them away, lay waiting anxiously with their eyes searching the mob.

"This is going to be tough, feller," Mexone confided to the Nuzian crouched beside him. "Once they realize we've run out of ammunition they'll make a mass attack…"

His eyes searched the sky desperately, hoping, as did Viona, for some sign of the spaceship. So far nothing so pleasant was visible…

Fortunately, the pile of metal from the gun was an ample protection, and the wariness of the Nuzians—after losing so many of their number—took up further time. Then, gradually realizing that all opposition had collapsed they fired their guns with withering force, beams flashing in all directions, chipping metal from a dozen different points.

The din of their cries made the clearing echo—then it was gradually obliterated by another noise, the glorious roar of rocket tubes! In a sudden rush their spaceship appeared over the glade, circled it twice, then let loose its incinerator rays. Screaming, yelling, the Nuzians tore pell mell for safety with burniing tracks whipping on their heels.

Mexone and Viona stared upward, waving their arms frantically. Thania's amplified voice bawled down at them.

"Put yourselves on that heap of gun metal—and better bring Vilji with you. I'll use the attractors and lift the lot!"

Mexone nodded, clutched the wet coldness of the Nuzian to him and scrambled up alongside Viona on the pile of dissembled gun. Inside three minutes the powerful grapple magnets of the ship descended, clutched the metal in its magnetized maw and lifted the trio upward to the ship's belly. The rest was easy... In a few minutes they were in the control room and the floor airlock dosed securely...

"Nice going!" Viona said approvingly, and Mexone smiled and affectionately ruffled the teenager's hair.

"Well, we made it... Next thing to do is to get into space and assemble the gun on the ship's exterior—on the roof. Gravity from the ship and magnetic anchors will hold it in position. Thania—take us out of here and into orbit!"

Thania skillfully piloted the craft up from the planet, and out into space. She established the ship in an orbit five hundred miles above Nuz, then cut the engines.

Quickly Mexone donned his space suit and scrambled through the emergency lock in the roof. Gaining the top of the ship he attached his lifeline and unbuckled the belt of instruments about his waist. It was a queer sensation standing thus on the hurtling vessel in the deeps of space, with sheer nothing on every side of him, and Nuz rolling away into the gulf below.

Accustoming himself gradually to a balance he went to work, drawing up the plates as, released from the anchor and held only by the ship's own gravity, they floated around the vessel...

The lack of gravity helped him in the assembling for one thing: for another it was a drawback because of the tendency for the plates to fly away from him. However, he kept on doggedly, fitting section into section so that the thing was horizontal, parallel with the ship's upper surface.

Nor did he manage it all in one sweep. Four times he rested: four times he worked—but at the end of the fourth effort it was completed, matrix in position, and potential solar power cylinder fully wired and reposing in the control room below. As for 'fuel' for the matrix he stuffed it with copper filings. Satisfied, he came back below.

"All we have to do now," he said, pulling off his space suit, "is point the ship the way we want the gun to fire: we're all set for aim…" He broke off and looked through the port. "How long before that asteroid comes within range?"

"About 70 minutes," Viona said, studying the radar equipment, and making a quick calculation.

"We'll break out of orbit and intercept it before it gets here," Mexone decided. "Lay a course, Viona—" He stopped and gave a yell.

"Hey there! Lay off!"

His order was directed to Vilji who was fingering the culture jar in which swarmed the deadly life they had taken from the asteroid after their first encounter.

Mexone hurried over. "Don't you realize this stuff is the very disease which struck down your race so long ago?" he demanded.

The Nuzian put the culture jar down slowly, pulled away his two fingers that had been immersed in the fluid. There was an odd look in his huge eyes.

"I thought—it might be," he said slowly.

Mexone turned purposely. "Time to get busy! We'll need to get into our protective suits again. Can you fetch them Thania? We'll soon be within range of the asteroid."

The girl hurried off and returned with four suits. They scrambled into them quickly, Mexone helping Vilji into the spare one, and switching on his communicator. Then Viona sent the ship sweeping ever nearer the deadly asteroid.

Mexone waited with his hand on the potential cylinder switch as the maneuvers went on. At last the nose of the ship was directly pointed at the asteroid…

He closed the power switch, sending the terrific force streaming into the matrix of the gun on the roof.

There was a brief stabbing ray, then a violent recoil that jerked the vessel with terrific force, sent them all sprawling. At the same instant an explosion glared space from somewhere outside, transmitting its concussion through the ship.

Hastily Mexone got up and switched off, looked at the others in baffled wonder. He scowled for a moment inside his helmet, then bundling on his space suit over his protective coverings he went up once more through the emergency lock. When he came back his face was unusually grim.

"We're beaten!" he announced briefly. "The gun's failed us!"

"But what's wrong?" Viona asked in dismay.

"For one thing the recoil has torn it away from the anchor hold and it is floating comparatively free. For another, there's a crack in the matrix casing, which lets power escape and gives us only twenty five percent down the gun barrel. I half expected it—it's the work of those blasted Nuzians when they attacked us! One of their rays weakened the casing and under sudden strain it fissured."

Viona and Thania couldn't find words to say: they were too stunned.

"That was our last throw of the dice," Mexone shrugged. "And it might have worked—but for the damage inflicted in our fight. Now we've nothing to prevent those molds falling to Nuz and spreading death among Vilji's race—"

He stopped rather impatiently as Vilji tugged him. He had his communicator in action. "Can I—look at gun? Outside?"

Mexone stared at his little face behind the visor. "I guess so. But what in heck can you do?"

"Idea," Vilji said simply. "Help me with space suit, please."

Mexone puzzled for a moment, then he nodded and stripped off his own space suit, and helped Vilji into it, checking that the air supply was working.

Vilji struggled into the suit, seeming to take a particular interest in the belt instruments. Finally he went up through the emergency lock, leaving the Crusaders watching him in puzzled silence through the roof port. He seemed to be fiddling with his belt.

Presently something gleamed in his hand.

"It's his knife," Mexone said in wonder. "What the hell does he think he can do with that, I wonder? He must have gone crazy!"

"Not crazy, friend Mexone…" Vilji's voice came over the communicator in his helmet. "You saved my life. I save yours. See culture jar. I prefer it this way. Have no planet worthwhile. So will die of service."

With a sudden sweep of his knife he slashed right through the lifeline holding him. Instantly the superior gravity of the deadly asteroid lifted him upwards—or rather downwards—hurtled him head over heels through the void, faster and faster, towards that glowing gray and merciless surface.

"He's broken loose!" Viona screamed. "He's—"

"Wait!" Mexone snapped. "He hasn't finished—Look!"

As he keeled into the growing remoteness they saw his knife flash once more. Instantly the remains of his space suit and protective coverings burst open. His body, dead certainly, broke free and hurtled faster and faster, tattered ends of garment fastened to it.

The body vanished in distance, but in their imaginations the Crusaders thought they saw the faint disturbance he made as he fell a lifeless wreck into that mass of mold.

"The fool! The little idiot!" Viona groaned. "He did that deliberately! Committed suicide! But why?"

"He mentioned the culture jar," Mexone said. "We'd better take a look at it, though I don't see where it fits in—"

Followed by Viona and Thania he hurried over to the jar of molds the Nuzian had been examining. Mexone whipped it up, tapped it—but to his amazement and that of the onlookers the feathery stuff remained motionless at the jar's base. It did more; it slowly disintegrated into powdery sediment.

Hurriedly Mexone fished out some of the stuff onto the slide, stared at it through the microscope.

"It's dead!" he whispered incredulously. "But—but—"

"Wait a minute!" Viona cried, thinking. "Didn't Vilji have his fingers in the fluid when we spoke to him? His forefingers?"

"I guess so—" Mexone started. "Good grief, Viona, you mean the disease he'd got, caused by solar activity, was fatal to this mold?"

"Why not?" Viona said. "A malignant disease to cure another form of malignant disease. Isn't that the basis of all serums and antitoxins? And that heroic little devil, realizing his disease could kill the mold, realized also what his whole body could do."

"You mean," Mexone breathed, "that he sacrificed himself in order that the stuff might die—that it might form a cancer capable of smashing it?"

"Yes... it's the only answer!"

Mexone stared before him. "Can you imagine the courage of that little guy...?"

The same thought in their minds the Crusaders hurried to the window and stared down. The judgment of Vilji had plainly been correct, for even as they watched they could see a brownish area beginning to spread from the bottom right hand limb of the asteroid. Quite obviously the blight was progressive, would quickly spread over the entire mold-surface and destroy that foul life forever.

"All that Nuz will get now is a brief rain of meteors when the asteroid breaks up on impact with that planet's atmosphere," Viona summed up. "We know from our previous unsuccessful efforts with the heat ray that the mold-vampire would almost certainly have survived the fiery heat of re-entry. It would have reached the surface undamaged—there to wreak havoc on the inhabitants. But not now it's been killed stone dead—thanks to the courage of Vilji."

Mexone nodded. "His quick thinking has given the Nuzians a chance to climb out of their present lowly state and, in time, regain their once-great civilization. The very fact that we found someone like Vilji amongst their number shows that they've maybe turned the corner."

There was a moment's silence as everyone considered that fact; then Mexone gave a last look at the asteroid, before turning away decisively. "Release our manual control and let the computers take over for our final hop to the Ultra, Viona. Our job here is completed."

"Aren't we going to stay long enough to see the asteroid crash back to Nuz?" Thania asked, a note of disappointment in her voice.

"Can't be done, youngster," Mexone responded. "We've already delayed our mission to the Ultra because of the time we've spent in this system. Whilst I'm pretty certain—in fact, positive—that Abna and the Amazon will have prevented Karg following us, I don't want to delay any further. It's tempting fate to leave the Ultra unattended and drifting in space for longer than we can help. I only hope it's still there...Viona?" he turned to look towards his wife who was busy at the control panel, to which was affixed the object compass.

"Yes, it's still in more or less the same position—allowing for Galactic Drift in the interval since we left Earth, that is," Viona replied, studying the instrument. "I've programmed the necessary adjustment into the computers, and the automatic pilot will do the rest. We'll align ourselves to the Ultra and start to build up our speed very shortly."

"Then let's get to the acceleration bunks," Mexone said decisively, taking Thania's arm as she still hesitated, staring out of the observation window onto the now brown, and totally dead, surface of the asteroid.

"I feel sort of guilty, just leaving that little hero's body lying there," Thania said contritely. "Shouldn't we do something?"

"What *can* we do?" Mexone asked patiently. He put an arm around her shoulder and gave a sympathetic smile at Thania's expression. "We've absolutely no idea of his religious beliefs—if any—and it seems to me that the best thing we can do for him is to leave him where he is. In due course he'll be cremated, when that asteroid strikes the super dense atmosphere of Nuz. And…and his ashes will be scattered across the surface of his home world. Don't you think that's appropriate?"

Thania nodded. "I suppose it is, at that." She brightened. "Maybe something he'd anticipated and would have appreciated."

CHAPTER SEVEN

Almega

The day was uneventful save for occasional showers of amazing rapidity, and a certain cooling of the air that could only be explained by the amazing Chameleon Planet's rapid orbital recession from the Sun.

During the brief two-hour day there were multi-alterations, and when the night fell again it was alive with change.

The two listened apprehensively to a myriad unfamiliar noises—the screech of unknown birds as they flew close over the camp; the monstrous, avid bellowing of 40-ton beasts—the ground-shaking concussions of their colossal feet. Somewhere something chattered with the hysterical abandon of a hyena.

At brief intervals the two slept from sheer strain and fatigue, until near the time for dawn when they were aroused by a sudden deep bass rumbling in the ground.

"Whatever is it?" the Amazon gasped in alarm, leaping up. "Sounds like an explosion of some kind…"

She jumped to the door and wrenched it open. Outside, rain was descending in hissing, blinding sheets. "More like an earthquake," came Abna's sober voice from the gloom. "Here—grab the provisions and pack in case we have to make a dash for it!"

He snatched at the Amazon's baggage and thrust it on her shoulders, but almost before he had slipped into his own equipment they were both flung off their feet by a terrific earth tremor.

"It's that zig-zag deviation in this planet's orbit!" Abna gasped, scrambling up again. "We must have reached it. Let's get out of here quick, before the whole camp comes down on top of us!"

"But where do we go?" the Amazon asked helplessly. "It's raining a deluge outside—"

"Can't help that!" he returned briefly, and hugging her to him they plunged out into the raging dark.

Lucky it was that his foresight had guided him, for they had hardly gained the clearing's center before another tremendous convulsion of the earth overthrew them. A visible ripple raced along the ground in the dawn light, ploughed down swaying trees and shelter in one all-inclusive sweep.

Raging, cyclonic wind gripped them as they staggered helplessly towards the rain-lashed jungle. Clutching each other, soaked to the skin, they were whirled along in the midst of crashing trees and ripping, tearing plants. The whole planet seemed to have suddenly gone insane.

Simmering volcanic forces had abruptly come into life, undoubtedly created by that orbit deviation swinging the globe out of normalcy.

Panting and drenched they halted finally in the jungle's depths, crouching down in the rain-flattened bushes as a herd of crazed animals thundered past. Mighty brutes, overpowering in their mad hugeness. It was a vast parade of armor plates, horns, laniary teeth, beaks and claws—the stampeded herd of an incredible saurian age on the verge of yet another weird metamorphosis.

"What do we do next?" the Amazon panted, as the earth heaved violently beneath them.

"Only stop as we are until we get a break!" Abna looked worriedly at the sky. Not only was it thick with lowering rain clouds but there also drifted across it the thick acrid smoke columns of volcanic eruption. Somewhere a crater had burst into being.

He turned back to the Amazon with a remark, but at that exact moment there came a roaring and crashing from the jungle to the rear. He was just in time to see a vast wall of water plowing forward, bearing everything before it in a towering deluge of driftwood and tumbling vegetation—then he and the Amazon, clinging frantically to each other, were lifted on high and hurled wildly into the foaming chaos.

They went deep, locked tightly in each others' embrace, rose up again gasping and struggling for air, threshing wildly in the driftwood as the weight of their packs pulled upon them. In the half light it was difficult to distinguish anything.

On every hand there was din and confusion; the piercing shrieks of drowning monsters split the screaming air.

"O.K.?" Abna yelled, clutching the Amazon to him, and she nodded her plastered head quickly.

"Yes—but I could think of better places to play water polo—What's that ahead? Land?" She stared through the smother.

"Of sorts," Abna threw back—and in three minutes they struck shelving ground from which all traces of forest had been blasted by earthquake and tempest.

For a space they could do nothing but lie flat on their

backs and gasp for breath, staring at the clearing sky—then little by little it came home to them that the earthquake and tidal wave were spent.

The heaving and trembling had ceased: the mad little world was itself again. For the first time sunshine filtered down through the densely packed clouds, gathering strength and intensity until the wet ground was steaming with the intense heat.

The Amazon sat up at last and thankfully lowered the pack from her back.

"Well thank Heaven neither water nor space can get through these," she remarked gratefully. "We can still survive a bit longer, though I certainly have a lurking suspicion that it isn't going to be easy to find our spaceship after this! Incidentally, Abna, doesn't it seem to you that it almost matches up—in a shorter version—with the Deluge and terrific re-patterning Earth underwent in the early stages?"

He nodded rather gloomily, staring out over the newly formed ocean.

"Very like it," he admitted. "Nature's law operating in a slightly different way—eliminating vast numbers of the giant beasts and permitting only a few to remain. Since they possess the powers of adaptation without death or heredity they will presumably pattern themselves on a smaller scale now. Everything large will probably have passed away—those things that resembled the dinosaurs, ichthyosauri and pterosaurs of Earth."

The Amazon made a wry face. "Thanks for the natural history lesson!" she murmured, scrambling to her feet. "Still, I believe you're right. Seems to me we'd better move before some sort of sun fever gets a hold on us, though at the rate this place moves, I hardly think it's possible to get ill— Well, what do you know about that!" she finished in astonishment, and pointed to the flat plain behind them.

Abna rose beside her and stood gazing in amazement. The plain was no longer a barren mass but was already thickly wooded in the glare of sunshine, backed at the rear by a newly risen mountain range. They stood looking on foliage that was vaguely familiar, almost Earth like— which, considering the planet's resemblance to the home world wasn't very surprising.

Dark plane trees, waving oaks, beeches—they were all sprouting and growing upwards rapidly. Amidst the branches there flitted the first signs of birds, the first visible feathered things. A steady humming presently proceeded from the forest—the low and ordered note of bees, dragonflies, moths, butterflies, and here and there as they watched a stinging specimen of the arthropod genus came into mystic being, chirped loudly, and sped swiftly away into the sunny silences.

"Do things move on this planet!" Abna whistled at length, tentatively fingering his gun. "An hour or two ago they were giant monsters; now they've changed again and resolved into the smaller classes— And look at that!" he finished, in a yell of amazement.

The Amazon hardly needed his directions. Her eyes were already fixed in astonishment upon a profusion of scampering but none the less recognizable creatures. There were marsupials, waddling armadillos, changing even as they were watched, with incredible swiftness into rodents and hoofed animals. The birds too, as they flew, merged astoundingly into new specimens, slipped swiftly by wild mutations into bats and insect-eaters.

"Pretty little playmates!" the Amazon murmured at last. "I guess we might take a closer look. We're literally between the devil and the deep sea, so what about it?"

Abna nodded. The sun was already curving down swiftly towards the horizon. Very soon it would be night. The forest for all its wild and peculiar life was a safer and more understandable proposition. There was no telling but what leviathans might emerge out of the ocean at the coming of nightfall.

They turned and strode forward purposefully. When they reached the forest it seemed to have already attained maximum limit, yet despite its dense profusion, only blasted clear by the flame guns, it was nowhere near the solid impregnability of the earlier jungles—was more natural, more beautiful, sub-tropical.

Darkness fell with its usual blanketing suddenness. Afraid to pause the two went on steadily, beheld things they could not have thought possible. Rats of astounding size occasionally flitted across their vision: some attempted to attack until they were shattered to dust with the guns. In other directions unclassifiable monstrosities lurked in the twisted grass, stared out with great diamond-like eyes or scuttled away into the friendly blackness. The whole place was infested with weird life, some very Earthly, some very alien.

Once, as the flashlight circled a wall of vegetation ahead, the two caught a vision of a ridiculous thing like an ostrich running away from them in sudden fright, its bushy tail standing up like an earthly cauliflower.

"A dinoris, or something very like it," Abna commented. "A forerunner of a future ostrich. Like—"

He stopped dead, muscles tensed and hand tightening

on his flame gun as a pair of fiendishly malevolent green eyes blazed suddenly ahead. A body of brilliant stripes moved through the quivering changing-grass.

"Saber-tooth tiger—a genuine pip!" he whispered, clutching the Amazon to him to halt her advance. "No time to take chances. Here goes!"

He fired his gun mercilessly at the very instant of the magnificent creature's spring. It never ended its leap; simply puffed into ash in mid-air.

"I hate to think what would happen if the guns gave out," the Amazon breathed. "To be unarmed in this place is to be dead."

She fell silent again as they resumed the advance. By the time they had passed through the thick of the jungle and reached the base of the mountain range beyond, the dawn had come again. But it was colder, much colder, and the sun seemed smaller…

For a time they wandered through the midst of loose rocks, finally singling out a cave opening in the sheer wall of towering diff. Weary and exhausted they crawled within and flung themselves down in relief, gazing back through the opening towards the rioting confusion of jungle a mile away, and, further away still, the ocean born of the tidal wave.

"Before very long all this will pass away and maybe we'll glimpse something of modernity—something that thinks, something that will explain why this planet behaves so queerly," Abna said musingly. "All the same, I think my own ideas are pretty correct."

The Amazon gave a yawn. "Well, theory or no theory I'm going to take a rest. We need to be fully rested and alert to survive."

They both pulled off their packs and squatted down. "You get some sleep, Vi. I'll take the first watch and wake you later," Abna said, his flame pistol ready as instant protection—but before very long fatigue got the better of even his mighty physique and, like the girl, he slept soundly.

* * * *

When they awoke again it was to the knowledge that, according to their watches, two nights and two days had slid by. The cave was unchanged. Once they had refreshed and eaten they crept to the opening and stared out onto the jungle.

It was different once again—still more refined but still primeval. Here and there the first new life forms were moving: bullet-like hairy beings shot from tree to tree with terrific speed. The ape evolution had been gained, was speeding onwards up the scale in absolute unison with the chameleon planet's gradual withdrawal from the sun.

"If this evolutionary scale is similar to Earth's we ought to get another Glacial Epoch around here," the Amazon murmured musingly. "It's a good job we brought space suits with us. It's getting pretty cold even as it is."

"There won't be a Glacial Period," Abna said with certainty. "Earth's ice age was mainly responsible for the final extinction of the saurians, but here they require no extinction: they simply merge into something fresh like a tadpole metamorphosing into a frog. Those distant apes we can see will be men before we can hardly realize it. Remember that by normal evolution millions of years passed in between states of change—but the speed of ascent from ape to man could be measured in mere thousands of years. That's why it should also go quicker here."

"In the meantime we stop right here then?"

"Certainly we do—it's a safe spot. Why shouldn't we?"

"I was thinking of the spaceship."

Abna laughed forlornly. "Nice thought that is! Probably it went west in the earthquake. But even if it did there will soon be life on this amazing world quite capable of building us a new one. You can count on that."

The Amazon became silent, staring moodily through the cave opening—then she suddenly stiffened and cried sharply.

"Look down there, Abna! A couple of apes fighting it out to the death! And the smaller one's getting the worst of it, too!"

He joined her in gazing, studied the mighty hairy forms that had emerged from the forest and were battling savagely with bare hands and fighting fangs for the possession of a piece of quivering animal flesh. The speed they fought at made them mere blurs of motion. And even as they fought they were changing swiftly. The heads were broadening out; the teeth and prognathous jaws projecting less.

Finally, the smaller of the two fell backwards, to be immediately pounced upon by the larger. At that Abna jumped to his feet, flame pistol tightly gripped in his hand.

"What's the idea?" the Amazon asked in a startled voice.

"A thought's just struck me, Vi. We could do with a companion from this world to tell us what it's all about. I'm going to rescue the smaller ape, if I can. Before long he'll be a man. Stay here or come with me. Please yourself."

She scrambled to her feet indignantly at that and followed him through the cave opening. Running swiftly together over the loose rubble they gained the fighting pair at last and paused, momentarily appalled by the overpowering fury and speed of the brutes. Beyond doubt it was a fight to the death. The forest behind was echoing with the gibbering of apes, sub-humans, and queerly fashioned things that had no identifiable origin, scuttling wildly through the fastness.

Abna hesitated for a moment, maneuvering for a good position—then as the giant aggressor abruptly stood upright for a final plunge Abna fired his flame gun. Vivid streaking energy struck the brute clean in the stomach, blasted his great hairy body into fragments amidst a passing stench of singeing hair and flesh.

"Nice shot!" the Amazon breathed, then swung round as the other ape got painfully to its feet.

By the time it had fully stood up it was miraculously healed of its injuries and had become less apelike in form, less shaggy. Instead it had all the evidences of an Earthly Heidelberg man—huge, hairy and terrible.

Abna backed away gently, flame gun ready, calling to the biped coaxingly.

"We're friends. Want to help," he said anxiously. "Don't try and start anything or we'll have to defend ourselves."

A momentary silence fell. Even the forest went quieter—changing and sliding strangely into new and complex patterns, whirling in the sea of mutations.

The rescued apeman stood in puzzled bewilderment, grinning diabolically. The Amazon, her own gun drawn, stared tensely at the sight of that receding forehead, protruding eyebrows, iron hard jaws and sharply pointed ears.

"Couldn't you have chosen a better looking pupil?" she commented dryly. "He's making me uneasy."

"As long as we've got our flame guns we're safe

enough…"

Abna held out his hand slowly, then snatched it back as the brute's huge teeth bared in petulant anger… Then suddenly it raised a hand to its little forehead and seemed to give the slightest of shudders. When it lowered the hand the facial appearance had changed again into that of a near-Neanderthal man.

Abna tired of the mutual scrutiny at last, tired of guessing at the workings in the creature's little brain. "Let's go, Vi." He turned, pointed towards the cliff cave, and headed back towards it, glancing ever and again over his shoulder.

"Maybe he'll follow," he murmured, and the girl frowned.

"I don't fancy being bottled up in a cave with that brute," she commented. "Personal hygiene doesn't seem to be his forte."

"Don't you get it yet? One day he'll be a man of supreme and far reaching intelligence," Abna snapped. "At the rate he changes at he'll be equal with you and me at the end of a few days. Besides he'll be darned helpful to us. He owes us a debt, don't forget. We saved his life."

The Amazon glanced back over her shoulder. "Well he's following us anyhow," she said. "Suppose we stop outside the cave? Maybe it'll be safer."

Abna nodded assent and once they gained the cave he stood ready and waiting until the brute came up. There was something incredible and baffling about the mad evolution of the creature. The sub-human effect had changed again: the creature had lost the power of operating the nodules of its simian-pointed ears. At terrific speed he was developing into an intelligent man.

Finally he came level, looking in almost childlike wonderment at his outspread fingers. Between them reposed the vestigial remains of his saurian origin. In thirty seconds they had become natural fingers, but thickly stubbed.

"We're trying to help you," Abna said presently, making dumb motions. "We want you for a friend."

The brute looked up; a faint flash of wisdom crossed his apish face and then disappeared. His only response was a deep, chesty grunt, then he sat down heavily right across the cave entrance as though to wait.

"No dice," Abna growled. "He *would* choose that place to squat. Guess we'll have to wait until he gets more intelligent."

The Amazon, her tenseness abating somewhat at the evidence of the creature's docility, squatted down too. Within a few minutes the sun dipped in the west over the fantastic forest, sinking at lightning speed.

The brute slept during the two-hour night, watched ceaselessly by the chilled and wondering Crusaders... When the sun rose again the creature was no longer an ape but a naked man quite on a par with a modern earth being.

The moment he woke up and beheld the two Crusaders watching him he leapt lithely to his feet and sped at a terrific speed into the distance—not towards a forest but towards an area now sprouting with rudely designed huts and abodes.

The age of the wild had passed.

"Pity he dashed off like that," was the Amazon's comment, as she rose stiffly and rubbed her chilled bare arms. "Maybe he got self conscious at finding himself a nudist. If he was as cold as I am I'm not surprised."

"The cold is our growing distance from the sun," Abna said. "As to our friend, the need for clothing, in his now advanced mind, will be a strong urge. I'm betting it won't be long before he turns up again!"

"Let's grab a meal whilst we have the chance," the Amazon and after diving into the cave for the provision bag she settled herself to eat and wait again, grateful for the sun, smaller though it undoubtedly was.

For an hour there was no sign of the ape-cum-man. The only changes lay in the queer city. With every passing moment it changed indescribably. Illusory flutterings constantly rippled over it. In fifteen minutes the crude dwellings were normal edifices; the first ramifications of a city were coming into being.

"Do you think that city builds itself or is it actually erected by the labor of unseen creatures?" the Amazon asked at last, her violet eyes utterly perplexed. "It isn't even reasonable to suppose that any beings could work at such a frantic rate and with progression of ideas."

"Don't forget that this planet is now in top gear," Abna murmured. "Think back on the terrific speed at which everything has moved—or at least it's looked that way to our senses. Remember the speed of the earlier metamorphoses, the whirling rate of that ape fight—the way our naked friend streaked off like lightning with the lid off. Because Earthly evolution and movement is so slow it doesn't imply that the same thing must exist everywhere else. This chameleon planet has to cash in on the fruits of an entire existence in the equivalent of a mere Earthly fortnight. That means that the inhabitants work in like ratio—don't even waste time on dying. Just grow right up from beginning to end. Their buildings appear like blurs because of the rate they move at. The further on evolution and intelligence travel the faster everything will go,

I expect. Increasing knowledge and modernity makes for increasing speed. What really interests me is where it is all going to end. Maybe Almega will be able to tell us if he comes back."

"Almega?" the Amazon asked in surprise, frowning.

"Yes—Alpha and Omega cut short. Suits him, don't you think?"

"Not bad—for you," the Amazon admitted with a faint smile; then before she could speak further there came a streak of dust from tumult of the city.

Out of the sunshine there suddenly emerged the figure of Almega himself, half smiling, now a complete man of an ultra-modern age.

A one-piece garment, blue in color and plastic in texture—specially designed to accommodate the constant changes of his figure—covered him from heels to neck. In his hands was what looked like a small metallic box.

Abna gave a start of surprise. "We're friends," he began again. "I tried to tell you when you were in primordial form—"

Almega thrust the box into Abna's hands, depressed a switch on its side, then disappeared the way he had came, leaving a faint trail of dust.

CHAPTER EIGHT

Ultra evolution

Abna almost dropped the box as he heard a voice speaking in English. It was cold and clipped, with an odd intonation, but perfectly understandable. "Impossible to communicate with you directly," said the voice. "I am so fast and you are so slow. This sound recording is mechanically slowed down more than a thousand fold, so as to be audible to you.

"Our evolution is very rapid. Soon I shall be what you would term a superman. Then on to other states. I leave this recording device with you in order to thank you for saving me and, although you did not know it, my entire race and planet! Thanks to you, I have lived to become the greatest scientist of our people, and together with my fellow scientists, I have devised a means of saving this planet from the destruction that otherwise awaits it.

"You saved my life when I was in primordial form. My brain was not then developed to its present stage. My brain was then only 430 grams. Now it is 1,350 grams. Soon it will be 2000 grams, and my body will change to accommodate it...

"As my brain developed I was able to read your minds and learn your simple language. I have sensed your puzzlement about my world, and so I will tell you something of our history—and what is to become of us.

"You have already glimpsed part of the truth. Time for us in our enclosed system is far swifter than it is to you from outside. Our evolution is encompassed in one circling of our sun—we go from beginning to end without dying and leave cellular spores at the end of our course, to start again at perihelion. Our climate too pursues the same changes, though of course it is an inactive state. Rain and sun here are so swift to you that you will hardly see the difference, save in the long disaster at the erratic point of this planet's orbit, which you have already experienced. Our flora and fauna resemble those of your Earth because of similar conditions.

"When we have run this present course of mankind, our world will not be empty. Man's stage only represents one dominion. Will be same on your world in the future. I see from your minds that your world is very far away. No matter. Man on any planet is only one form of dominion. Before that stage we were the masters in other forms. Just as there have been former types, so there will be later types. Incessant change. Shortly I shall lose sense of smell and develop spectroscopic eyes and ears. I shall read the light-symphonies of Nature; I shall hear the pulsations of the universe. My teeth will disappear, so will my hair. My eyes' visual range will change as this world speeds further away from our sun and becomes embraced in twilight. As the dark deepens I shall see in that, too. Ears will disappear. We shall conquer all things as Man—so swiftly you will not see it. We shall conquer space and the universe. To you a mere blur. Evolution will go on…

"Over millions of years, my planet has been slowly

drifting ever closer to what you term a black hole. Seeping through it from the alternate universe on its other side is a form of alien energy that is completely outside this universe's electromagnetic spectrum. Indeed it would have to be, otherwise it could not escape from the black hole's gravity well, which seals up every known form of energy and matter. This seepage is the source of our dilated time, and the reason for our strange evolution. But now my astronomical calculations have shown that this world is finally about to cross what you term the Swartzchild Radius, and will be drawn into the black hole at the end of this present orbit. However, my fellow scientists and I have devised a means of turning this coming disaster into the means of our salvation!

"Several times in the past, in earlier cycles, my ancestors have mastered space travel, even as you yourselves have done, and have attempted to migrate into outer space, away from the influence of the black hole. They hoped that in another solar system they might remain at the peak of human evolution, and perhaps go even further and reach their ultimate potential, instead of inevitably slipping back into a primordial state.

"Alas for their hopes! Once outside the space-time warp which encloses this system, their bodies withered and crumbled into dust! Their bodies, in normal space-time, were millions of years old, and so entropy caught up with them in a single devastating stroke! It seemed that our race was doomed to remain in this looped system forever...

"But now we face death and destruction in the black hole, unless I can save the planet—and I believe I can do just that.

"We believe that the hole forms a gateway into an alternate universe. In the different conditions in this reversed space-time continuum, our race can *continue* to evolve without slipping back to a primordial state! There we shall reach the ultimate stage of evolution—pure thought! We shall become as Gods in our new domain...

"Already our preparations are underway to protect out planet from being utterly crushed and consumed in the black hole. Everything has been thought out over centuries of study and work. Ordinarily, our atmosphere would be torn off by the tremendous gravity pull as we approached the hole: landscapes would collapse and seas spew forth into space ahead of our downward path. Human beings would be driven into the rocks by their own weight under the awful acceleration and gravity. Therefore, before this can happen, our entire atmospheric envelope will be impregnated with rods of force.

"There always exists in the upper atmosphere of any planet an encircling band of electricity, and electricity with the proper conductors can always be brought to the surface. So, the plan is to impregnate the entire atmospheric envelope, all over the world, with a special chemical of my own devising that will rapidly settle to the ground, covering land and sea in a fine cloud of gray, glittering dust. That is what I call earthing-dust.

"Once all this has settled—it will be distributed by high-powered wind machines—a current will be released from my laboratory into the air which will instantly cause the electrical bands in the stratosphere to shoot to the earthing-dust below. This will take the form of rods of fire, or force, at intervals of three hundred of your miles. Thus, atmosphere will be held securely intact by electrical power. The chemical has a life quite long enough for our purpose to be achieved."

Throughout the amazing scientific exposition, neither Abna nor the Amazon had spoken to each other. They listened intently, determined not to miss a word, occasionally flashing an amazed glance at each other. Abna had carefully lowered the recording box to the ground, and now they sat near to it, absorbing every word.

"At the same time as we create the earthing rods of force, we will create a shield of force around our planet, at the limit of the atmosphere. This will cut off all lines of force, including that of gravity. All phenomena are, at root, a variation of electromagnetic energy. We can create a field of force that will heterodyne anything emanating from the black hole, be it gravity or any other force, and protect our planet as we plunge through into—as we believe—this other universe where my race can survive and thrive.

"Initially, this will not be in human form. Before then, still subject to the vagaries of this universe and our closed system of continuous, circular evolution, we shall become insects. So it will happen with your world. Already your insects are adapted for future control. Particularly your *cephenomia* fly. It is the fastest flier on your planet. So will we be. We shall war with termites, gain brief mastery and change again. By then—to you mere days—our planet will have moved very far from our normal sun. It will be cold. We shall change into wormlike beings—*echinodermata,* as you call them. We shall go further than that; move into the state from which we came—a single cell. In that wise, still intelligent, we shall live through into the ultimate night of our world at aphelion. The cell will remain, to be born again at the planet's perihelion around the counterpart sun we shall find on the other side of the hole, and repeat the life-cycle. But only for one more time, and then we shall continue to evolve—but without reverting!

"I anticipate that you might be surprised at my mention of a single cell. But I have learned from your minds that you had a similar thing on your world in the alluvian epoch. You called it *Caulerpa*. It looked like green algae, had a fern-like body and grew to four feet in height. All in one cell.

"And the purpose behind this—to you—astounding evolution of ours? To live through all our stages and work back to a single cell, then to do it all again? My present fellows and I will not come again. When our intelligence passes at the planet's aphelion we shall go elsewhere, leaving behind only a cell, which at perihelion will sprout again. But with another mind. Where our own minds go we do not know. Like you we do not understand the riddle of death.

"The creation of the force screen and binding rods will be carried out automatically at the critical time by flawless machines, which we are constructing now. Already an epoch has gone during this recording," came the voice of Almega. "You must leave this planet immediately. As the saviors of my people we desire you to keep safe.

"Your space ship was not destroyed. I will return shortly to direct you to it. Reach it as soon as you can. This world will pass shortly to remote aphelion, before returning on a deflected path that will plunge it into the back hole. Cold will completely destroy you but we shall adapt ourselves.

"Your spaceship lies in a straight line in the direction I will indicate to you. My debt to you is now repaid. Farewell!"

There was a distinct clicking sound as the recording

ended. The Amazon flashed an anxious glance at Abna. "I don't like this! Things are now moving so fast around here, I don't see how it will be possible for us to even see Almega when he returns to give us directions, and—" She broke off at a sudden blurring flickering arrow of light and shade which approached them at lightning speed from the direction of the city, and then just as quickly reversed itself.

The Amazon followed the phenomenon's amazing progress, then turned as Abna burst out laughing. Right next to him was a metal post, driven firmly into the ground, and attached to the top of it was a single directional pointer.

Abna carefully checked its direction on his wrist compass. "Your problem solved, Vi!" he remarked admiringly. "Simple but ingenious use of an unmoving inanimate object, so that we'd be bound to see it. We didn't see Almega himself of course—unless you count that blurred streak of light.

"He can certainly move! I guess he could play badminton with himself and sleep between serves…!" Then Abna sobered a little as he glanced at the stern-faced Amazon. She rarely appreciated his whimsical humor in a tight situation.

"If you've no more jokes, Abna, we'd better get moving," she said tersely. "The air is already getting distinctly chilly."

They shouldered their packs again, cast a last look at the cave, then as they moved away from it darkness returned to Chameleon Planet.

* * * *

That night of all others was painted with sights unique in the Crusader's experience of planet exploration. As they moved sharply in the direction Almega had indicated—apparently due south by Abna's illuminated wrist compass—they beheld the transformation of the city in all its weird, incredible glory.

The scene presented was that of a blur of lights as buildings supplanted buildings, as the air machines of a now far-reaching science streaked the blackness. Sound, deep-pitched and vibrant, floated across the intervening space like the droning of a super beehive. It was hard to imagine that in that enormity of power and mutation a race was passing literal epochs.

The Crusaders only stopped twice during the night to rest. When the dawn came the city was behind them, momentarily still in its wild constructions. The chill wind of that dawn, the paling light of the increasingly distant sun, both embraced a city that had come to a stop, the ingenuity of architecture evidently at last played out. A row of tall, slender buildings reaching to the sky, atop which there stood complicated towers and the various electromagnetic devices of a far advanced science, stood in mute testimony to the slow passing of a race that had reached its mightiest thoughts—in man form at least—in two short hours of apparent night!

"We'd better wrap ourselves up a bit," the Amazon commented at length, rubbing her arms vigorously. "It's getting freezing cold. The air's thinning a bit, too. No telling yet how far we may have to go."

The night shut down like a breath from the void, sending them stumbling onwards with a slowly rising fear—the fear of unknown forces reaching out of that great and ebon dark. Afraid to stop, they kept on going.

The dawn was the strangest they had seen. The sun was as red and cold as that in Earth's Arctic Circle, so vast was its distance. Its long, slanting red wavelengths fell upon a forest directly ahead.

"Is—is it a forest?" asked the Amazon uncertainly through the helmet radio, stopping wearily. "I thought all life had gone for good."

They moved more slowly now, both from fatigue and the cumbersome folds of their space suits. In five minutes they gained the forest and passed into its slowly changing midst. It was so far the slowest and yet the most astounding place they had witnessed. A woodland of gray, frosty shapes, sheerly beautiful, deeply red lit. The life that tenanted it, harmless apparently, moved with a certain slowness... but *what* life!

Enormous reeds were gliding along through the thinning air like decapitated serpents, twisting and writhing, unutterably grotesque. In another direction bristling gray footballs were rolling swiftly along in search of hidden prey, propelled after the manner of an earthly polypus by whip-like tentacles.

As the Crusaders passed wonderingly through their midst, staring incredulously at the infinitely diversified forms, one or other of the strange objects burst suddenly apart and became two—bipartition of cells.

"Unicellular life of the *nth* degree," Abna breathed, fascinated.

"I'd sooner see a space ship than a whole lot of cells," the Amazon sighed. "How much further, I wonder?"

They went on slowly through the very midst of the balls and rods, through the thickest part of the lacy, cellular trees, until at length they were through it. Behind them, the forest began to disappear... Gigantic bacteria, the toughest, most adaptable things in life, were beginning the final dominion before the utter extinction of death itself.

Ahead there stretched a desert of ice. Nothing was stirring in that reddish lit bitterness: no new form of life was manifesting under the sheathed armor of what had once been land and water. Chameleon Planet was on the verge of death.

The Amazon stopped suddenly and gripped Abna's inflated arm.

"Suppose we never find the ship?" she asked quietly. "Do you realize what it means? This world is finished—and so will we be if something doesn't—"

She broke off. The sun, slanting swiftly down to the horizon, suddenly set something gleaming brightly not half a mile distant—a pointed spire in the ice field.

She jerked forward quickly, and then stopped dead, appalled at what she saw.

Abna too pulled up short on the ice as he saw the reason for her reaction.

It was the ship! Half of it projecting sharply out of the ice; the rest of it buried in the frozen tomb. As Abna hesitated, assessing possibilities, the Amazon whipped out her flame gun.

"Still a chance!" she panted. "The airlock's shut so the inside will be unharmed. It won't be crushed, either—the plates are strong enough to resist that ice pack. Get busy!"

Without further words they both set to work with their twin flame guns.

Tearing off her pack, the Amazon dived, perfectly protected by her space suit. She used her flame gun constantly to keep the ice from reforming and crushing her to death... To spin the external screws of the airlock was a matter of moments.

Her shout of triumph sounded in Abna's helmet radio as he too came floating through the narrow tunnel.

By degrees, working like divers, they shut the two safety compartment doors one after the other and finally gratefully gained the interior of the control room.

Still space-suited, the Amazon gave the power to the rocket tubes. The exhaust blasted ice and water in a vast shower. Abna slid into the control seat alongside her.

"Full power, Vi!" he said briefly. "Better get us away from here before Almega establishes that force barrier. Once he does that, we'll be hopelessly trapped on this planet—" He broke off with a grunt as acceleration slammed him deeper into his seat.

The spaceship climbed steadily, gained the stratosphere, then plunged into space. Barely seconds after they cleared the last vestiges of atmosphere, the planet below them became suffused with a coruscating patina of electrical energies.

There followed a long, tense period in which the Crusaders' vessel struggled to pull clear of the massive gravitational pull of the black hole. As the Amazon remained at the controls, Abna got up and operated the telescope, trained it back on the area of space where they knew the invisible black hole was present.

"Nothing visible, just the black of outer space," he murmured. "No—wait! I've got something…a tiny circular black patch just visible against that star field, and—yes, I can see Chameleon Planet! It's glowing like a bright star!"

"Then the electrical force shield is in still place," the Amazon muttered. "Good! That gives Almega and his race a fighting chance, at least…"

"It's gone!" Abna cried. "Disappeared! One second it

was there, the next—"

"Gone," the Amazon finished soberly. "Gone from this universe for ever. Into the black hole!" She broke off, as an instrument reading caught her eye. Then: "And we could be joining it!" she finished, her voice taut with anxiety.

CHAPTER NINE

The Final Paradox

"What!" Abna rejoined the Amazon, slipping into the control seat next to where she was seated, her face grim. "What are you talking about, Vi? It should be a simple job for us to pull clear—"

"Normally, yes. That is to say, if this ship had sufficient copper for fuel," the Amazon responded. "As it is our supplies have dwindled to danger level."

"But surely we have enough?" Abna questioned sharply. "Back on Earth, when General Milford laid this ship on for us, he'd hardly overlook that detail."

"He didn't," the Amazon said. "We had plenty of copper aboard when we took off. But don't forget that during our duel with Karg, we had to accelerate to near light speed. Then came our leap to hyper space—something we never anticipated. Then we had the prolonged deceleration when we emerged from hyper space, and then our catching up and landing on Chameleon Planet. All of that used up a terrific amount of fuel. And lastly," the Amazon finished, "we've expended a tremendous amount of fuel now in attempting to pull clear of the combined pull of Chameleon Planet and that black hole behind it! The planet's gone now, of course, and that may help—unless its mass has been added to the black hole!"

Abna studied the instrument readings. "We're only managing to move forward because we're still accelerating—albeit slowly. But if the fuel runs out before we're clear, we've had it! We'll be sucked back into the hole and we don't have Almega's force field—or any type of force field in this antiquated Earth ship—to protect us. But even if we do get clear, we won't have enough fuel to accelerate to light speed and get back to Earth to make our rendezvous with Viona in the returned Ultra."

"What fools we were!" the Amazon said bitterly. "We should have checked our fuel supplies the moment we emerged from hyper space after that plunge around the sun. If we had, we'd have scanned this planet for copper before landing, and made that our first priority before attempting to explore—"

"We can hardly blame ourselves for that, Vi. At the time we were both gripped by the sheer scientific mystery of the set-up."

"Well, now we're in real trouble," the Amazon said. "This system hasn't a single planet left, where we might have found copper. Probably it had in the remote past, but one by one any planets must have spiraled down into that black hole—Chameleon Planet was the last."

Both the Crusaders fell silent, as the Amazon sat rigidly at the controls, coaxing every bit of acceleration the ship could muster. The previous dull whine of the power plant took on an increasingly shrill note. Fascinated, Abna stared at the instrument readings, watching results, his knuckles white where his hand gripped the edge of the control panel.

As the power plant shrilled its song of defiance, the air in the control room became stale with a growing heat.

It was if the black hole was a sentient thing, a monstrous terrier that had gripped the ship in its jaws, and would not let it go.

Abruptly the sound of the power plant ceased and there was a sudden and complete silence.

Still without speaking, both Crusaders jumped up and hurried to the nerve center of the ship. The Amazon moved a switch, and a tv camera behind leaded screens showed the power matrix on a screen. They beheld the jaws of the main bar pressed into close contact, with no copper block between.

"The power block's been completely consumed!" the Amazon exclaimed. "And the fact that it hasn't been automatically replaced shows that we're right out of fuel! Without acceleration we'll start to fall back into the hole—"

"Emergency drill!" Abna snapped. "We've faced this problem before, and overcome it. We've got to ransack and strip the ship of all metal fitments, and use it in the power plant. Pure copper is the best fuel, but everything metallic can be made to release some atomic energy. You find what copper you can, I'll tackle the rest. Let's get busy!"

The Amazon set to work to find anything made of copper that could be used in the matrix of the atomic furnace. She ripped out terminals, earthing-rods, struts, wires, light switches—everything removable was torn to pieces, and finally welded at high temperature into a moderate sized copper cube. This she fixed in the jaws of the power plant and then dived back to the controls. The rockets began to fire again, slowing their descent, and moving the ship forward again.

Abna, meanwhile, was also behaving like a vandal, tearing away anything metallic that was not in immediate use, and throwing it into a pile on the floor. Lastly, using only his own main strength, he ripped out several stanchion bars, added them to the pile of smaller objects. Then he used the welding apparatus left by the Amazon to mold the lot into a fair sized rough cube. This was pushed into the shute leading to the power plant matrix. When the present copper was exhausted, the metal block would be released and slid into position.

Tensely he watched the tv monitor screen. The small copper cube the Amazon had put there was rapidly exhausted, and the rough metal cube was moved into position. Immediately the mass of metal began to glow brightly and commenced to shrink slowly. Abna dashed back to the control room and rejoined the Amazon.

Not being copper, the preferred fuel for providing atomic energy, the metal was being consumed at an alarming rate. Finally there came a moment when the last vestiges of metal had been consumed, and the fact was registered on the instrument panel. The Amazon turned a sweating face.

"That's it, Abna. Either we're out of the gravity well, and we'll continue to drift forward, or—"

"We're still being pulled back!" Abna yelled. "The instruments show it clearly!" The Amazon gave a start of surprise as Abna seized her roughly by the shoulders, bundling her out of the control seat.

"Into spacesuits, Vi, quickly! It's a last throw of the dice. I just might be able to metaphysically project us a distance into space, but—" He broke off as the Amazon suddenly began to shimmer, quickly becoming briefly transparent, before disappearing entirely!

Before Abna had time to guess at what was happening he felt his every nerve being twisted and wracked. Then abruptly he was not conscious of his body at all.

* * * *

Abna felt life tingling back through his body. He was breathing normally. Out of the oblivion of his thoughts objects began to come into the focus of his restored vision. Bright lights, winking instruments, shining metal surfaces. He found himself sitting up on a metal grid. A familiar smiling face was looking down at him. He accepted the extended hand and climbed to his feet.

"By all that's wonderful! Or am I dreaming?"

"Of course not, Abna. Can't you recognize our own daughter—not to mention the Ultra?" Abna shot a sideways glance at the sound of the Amazon's voice. She too was rising from where she had lain alongside him on the metal grid. Impatiently she disengaged her arm from the gentle grip upon it by Mexone, who had helped her to her feet. Then, bethinking herself, she gripped his hand in a quick handshake.

"Thanks," she said briefly, and nodded and smiled as she saw Thania coming forward from where she had been operating the electronic transit apparatus. "Atomic dissembly of course?" she asked.

"Yes," the teenager smiled. "It was the only way we could save you. You see, when we—"

The Amazon waved a hand, looked urgently at Viona and Mexone. "Explanations can wait. Get the Ultra out of here! It's important that we leave this system immediately."

Abna frowned. "Is that necessary Vi? In the Ultra we can easily stay clear of the black hole. I was thinking that it might be an interesting opportunity to study it, and..." He broke off at the Amazon's expression, and smiled ruefully.

He looked at Viona, who stood hesitating.

"Better jump to it, Viona. Your Mother's in one of her 'She-who-must-be-obeyed' moods!"

Viona smiled, then with Mexone and Thania in tow she turned and hurried to the control board, where they slid into their seats. The Amazon and Abna walked behind them, and sat down on one of the wall bunks.

Seconds later the mighty vessel was on the move, streaking through the void with increasing speed, heading away from the black hole. Within minutes it had also crossed the orbit of the normal sun, and was headed out of the binary system altogether, into the deeps of interstellar space.

Abna looked at the Amazon and raised an interrogative eyebrow.

The Amazon compressed her lips, then shrugged. "If you used your scientific gifts a little more, Abna, and your sense of whimsy less, we'd all be much safer!" she admonished. "Didn't it strike you as very strange indeed that the Ultra should turn up as it did, to save us?"

Before Abna could frame his answer, their trio of rescuers came over to join them. "But it wasn't strange at all, Mother," Viona interjected, smiling. "What happened was really quite simple. When we eventually reached the Ultra, we found it just as we'd left it, the airlock sealed, and everything untouched and undamaged…"

"*Eventually* reached it?" Abna questioned.

"We decided that we had a job to do first—as Crusaders—after we'd arrived in the target star system," Mexone explained. "A little matter of destroying a malignant vampiric life form on an asteroid. It was threatening all life on a nearby planet—Nuz by name."

Abna smiled. "Nothing too serious, then," he said dryly. "You were saying, Viona?"

"The very first thing we did—after examining the Ultra to make sure there were no unwelcome visitors on board—was to check your readings on the aura-compass." Viona paused and gave a slightly embarrassed smile.

"Whilst we were pretty confident that you would have easily have defeated Karg, I just wanted to be sure that you were both alive, and—"

"Actually we came very close to being killed," the Amazon said, and smiled faintly at Viona's expression of concern. "But go on with your story, my dear."

"Well, we were very surprised to get a reading that placed both of you in another stellar system altogether. We were expecting to find that you were still in the Earth solar system. Instead we discovered that you had left it, and traveled some 50 light years in the process!"

"Fortunately," Mexone put in, "you had traveled in more or less the same direction as we had, so you were that much nearer to us. We decided to make a single jump through hyper space, to reach you as quickly as we could."

"Why?" Abna asked, and this time it was Thania who answered.

"The only thing we could think of was that maybe Karg had escaped from the solar system, and that you were chasing him. We thought you might be able to use some help—"

"Imagine our surprise," Viona resumed, "when we emerged from hyper space to find ourselves in a binary star system, with one of them a black hole. When we consulted the aura-compass again, we were disconcerted to discover you were in a spaceship that was being drawn into the black hole! After that it was a simple matter to feed the compass readings into the atomic dissembler, and snatch you from the ship to safety aboard the Ultra."

"We certainly did need your help," Abna laughed. "If you hadn't have turned up exactly when you did, we'd have been in real trouble, and..."

"That's just *it*," the Amazon broke in impatiently. "Don't you see even yet?" She turned to look at Viona. "About how long were you in hyper space? In total—both in getting to the Ultra, and then reaching your father and I?"

Viona wrinkled her brow. "In total...including a couple of days on Nuz...I'd say about 10 weeks."

The Amazon gave Abna a sharp look. "We were in hyper space for just three days, before we reached Chameleon Planet. And we were on that planet for—"

"About two weeks!" Abna exclaimed, smiting his brow. "Sorry, Vi. Now I know I'm slipping... No wonder you wanted to get away from that black hole system! We were beginning to get affected by it! We were advancing through time ourselves!"

"Exactly." The Amazon permitted herself a faint smile. It pleased her to know that she had grasped a scientific truth before Abna had done so.

"Chameleon Planet had been subjected to the time distortion energy seeping from that black hole for millions of years," the Amazon said. "And its influence was greatest as it neared aphelion, doubling back in its orbit past the black hole. We were on it for only two weeks, and in that time—although we didn't realize it at the time—we were slowly beginning to be affected by it, and had moved ahead in time by some 8 weeks. Had we stayed there—and somehow stayed alive for another few million years—

we'd have become just like Almega and his fellows!"

Viona, Mexone and Thania had been listening to this exchange in growing bewilderment.

"Chameleon Planet?"

"Time distortion energy?"

"Almega?"

The Amazon smiled, and rose to her feet. "Let's all have a meal," she suggested. "We can each bring each other up to date on our recent adventures. I admit to being intrigued by Mexone's reference to a vampiric life form… I fancy we've both got quite a tale to tell!"

As the Crusaders ate, they talked. And the Ultra rushed soundlessly through space, in the heart of the Milky Way, heading towards…

Nobody knew.

The only thing certain was that if their recent experiences had been anything to go by, it was going to be something extraordinary!

MORE BORGO PRESS TITLES
BY JOHN RUSSELL FEARN

THE ADAM QUIRKE SERIES

The Master Must Die: A Science Fiction Mystery
The Lonely Astronomer : A Science Fiction Mystery

THE ANJANI SERIES

The Gold of Akada: A Jungle Adventure Novel
Anjani the Mighty: A Lost Race Novel

THE BLACK MARIA SERIES

Black Maria, M.A.: A Classic Crime Novel
The Murdered Schoolgirl: A Classic Crime Novel
One Remained Seated: A Classic Crime Novel
Thy Arm Alone: A Classic Crime Novel
Death in Silhouette: A Classic Crime Novel

THE HERBERT THE DINOSAUR SERIES

A Thing of the Past
The Genial Dinosaur

OTHER BOOKS

1,000-Year Voyage: A Science Fiction Novel
Account Settled: A Science Fiction Mystery

Before Earth Came: Classic Science Fiction Stories
Bury the Hatchet: A Crime Tale
A Case for Brutus Lloyd: A Science Fiction Mystery
The Crimson Rambler: A Crime Novel
Don't Touch Me: A Crime Novel
Dynasty of the Small: Classic Science Fiction Stories
The Empty Coffins: A Mystery of Horror
The Fourth Door: A Mystery Novel
From Afar: A Science Fiction Mystery
Fugitive of Time: A Classic Science Fiction Novel
The G-Bomb: A Science Fiction Novel
The Haunted Gallery: Crime Stories
Here and Now: A Science Fiction Novel
Into the Unknown: A Science Fiction Tale
Last Conflict: Classic Science Fiction Stories
Legacy from Sirius: A Classic Science Fiction Novel
The Man from Hell: Classic Science Fiction Stories
The Man Who Was Not: A Crime Novel
Manton's World: A Classic Science Fiction Novel
Moon Magic: A Novel of Romance (as Elizabeth Rutland)
One Way Out: A Crime Novel (with Philip Harbottle)
Pattern of Murder: A Classic Crime Novel
Reflected Glory: A Dr. Castle Classic Crime Novel
Robbery Without Violence: Two Science Fiction Crime Stories
Rule of the Brains: Classic Science Fiction Stories
Shattering Glass: A Crime Novel
The Silvered Cage: A Scientific Murder Mystery
Slaves of Ijax: A Science Fiction Novel
Something from Mercury: Classic Science Fiction Stories
The Space Warp: A Science Fiction Novel
The Time Trap: A Science Fiction Novel
Valley of Pretenders: Classic Science Fiction Stories
Vision Sinister: A Scientific Detective Thriller
Voice of the Conqueror: A Classic Science Fiction Novel
What Happened to Hammond? A Scientific Mystery
Within That Room!: A Classic Crime Novel
World Without Chance: Classic Science Fiction Stories

www.ingramcontent.com/pod-product-compliance
Lightning Source LLC
Chambersburg PA
CBHW020656180626
46816CB00003B/1316